Hunger gnawed at Abra

But it had nothing to do with the pizza she'd craved earlier. Sean was standing on her doorstep. His presence was tangible, so hard and male and tantalizing. He looked like sex on a stick dangled right in front of her.

She wanted this man. She wanted to grab him by the shirt and pull him into the bedroom.

Oh Lord, this was *so* not the time. Her new habit of popping into a state of instant arousal around him was so bizarre. Was it just the pregnancy that made her melt with need the minute she spotted a man with all the pieces in the right place? Or something else?

I have to get rid of him before it gets any worse, she thought wildly. *But he knows who I am.*

"I think you should leave," she said.

All he said gently was "We need to talk, Abra."

"Why? Looking for some more details for the tabloids?" she asked derisively, hoping that acting all mean would cool her sex drive.

Sean stood very still. There was an economy of motion around him she found appealing. Too appealing. And the way his hands jammed in his pockets pulled his jeans tighter across the front... *Oh, my god, don't stare at his uh—*

So much for self-control.

Dear Reader,

It's Harlequin Temptation's twentieth birthday and we're ready to do some celebrating. After all, we're young, we're legal (well, almost) and we're old enough to get into trouble! Who could resist?

We've been publishing outstanding novels for the past twenty years, and there are many more where those came from. Don't miss upcoming books by your favorite authors: Vicki Lewis Thompson, Kate Hoffmann, Kristine Rolofson, Jill Shalvis and Leslie Kelly. And Harlequin Temptation has always offered talented new authors to add to your collection. In the next few months look for stories from some of these exciting new finds: Emily McKay, Tanya Michaels, Cami Dalton and Mara Fox.

To celebrate our birthday, we're bringing back one of our most popular miniseries, Editor's Choice. Whenever we have a book that's new, innovative, *extraordinary*, look for the Editor's Choice flash. And the first one's out this month! In *Cover Me,* talented Stephanie Bond tells the hilarious tale of a native New Yorker who finds herself out of her element and loving it. Written totally in the first person, *Cover Me* is a real treat. And don't miss the rest of this month's irresistible offerings—a naughty Wrong Bed book by Jill Shalvis, another installment of the True Blue Calhouns by Julie Kistler and a delightful Valentine tale by Kate Hoffmann.

So, come be a part of the next generation of Harlequin Temptation. We might be a little wild, but we're having a whole lot of fun. And who knows—some of the thrill might rub off....

Enjoy,

Brenda Chin
Associate Senior Editor
Harlequin Temptation

JULIE KISTLER

CUT TO THE CHASE

*Happy
Reading!
Juli Kistler*

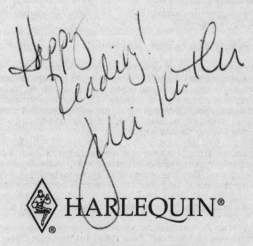

HARLEQUIN®

TORONTO • NEW YORK • LONDON
AMSTERDAM • PARIS • SYDNEY • HAMBURG
STOCKHOLM • ATHENS • TOKYO • MILAN • MADRID
PRAGUE • WARSAW • BUDAPEST • AUCKLAND

ISBN 0-373-69161-0

CUT TO THE CHASE

Copyright © 2004 by Julie Kistler.

This edition published by arrangement with Harlequin Books S.A.

® and TM are trademarks of the publisher. Trademarks indicated with
® are registered in the United States Patent and Trademark Office, the
Canadian Trade Marks Office and in other countries.

Visit us at www.eHarlequin.com

Printed in U.S.A.

A NOTE FROM THE AUTHOR...

If you read *Hot Prospect,* the first book in THE TRUE BLUE CALHOUNS trilogy, you already know that a stand-up guy with a badge can be a pretty sexy thing, in or out of uniform. Jake Calhoun, the oldest brother, stole my heart with his steady, stalwart ways. But when it came to Sean, the second brother... Whoa. Creating *Cut to the Chase* for Sean made the temperature rise around here!

Sean is more of a rebel, but he, too, knows when it's the right time to stand up and be counted. And that time turns out to be when he runs into Abra Holloway, a lifestyle expert and general "Miss Know-It-All" who's having trouble knowing anything for sure these days. On the run, in a whole lot of trouble, Abra needs a guy like Sean. And she certainly *wants* a guy like Sean. In fact, she can't stop wanting him. The two of them together turned out to be pretty combustible. I hope you agree!

And next month don't forget to look for little brother Cooper, who is *Packing Heat* as he continues the brothers' mission to look for the mysterious con woman who may be a) their illegitimate sister b) their father's mistress, or c) none of the above. Will reckless, good-time Cooper be the True Blue Calhoun to find the quarry?

I hope you're reading along to find out!

All the best,

Julie Kistler

Books by Julie Kistler

HARLEQUIN TEMPTATION
808—JUST A LITTLE FLING
907—MORE NAUGHTY THAN NICE
957—HOT PROSPECT

Dedicated to Birgit, for so many things,
including grace under pressure and many kindnesses

_____Prologue_____

ABRA SANK INTO A seat in the waiting area near her gate. She was ages early for her flight, and the place was deserted, with not even an agent behind the counter yet. Good. She could relax.

When she left the city, she'd rented a car and just driven blindly away, anywhere, finally dropping it in New Jersey. After that, she'd taken a train to Philly and a bus to Baltimore, and now she was flying to Chicago from there. It wasn't as if it would be hard to follow her trail, even though her hair was now a different color and cut, she had no makeup on, and she was wearing a baseball cap she'd just purchased in the concourse. No one in the world would expect Abra Holloway to have brown hair, let alone an Orioles baseball cap.

But to trail her, someone would have to want to. And who would want to?

She leaned back into her uncomfortable seat, clutching her boarding pass. Gone were the days when she flew first class and flight attendants brought her extra drinks and other passengers sneaked up from coach to ask for her autograph.

"Better get used to it. You're flying coach from now on," she told herself sternly, sticking the ticket back in her bag and pulling out a book to read till her flight.

But the book was about a dazzling television star with a terrible secret, and she couldn't imagine why she'd bought it. Who wanted to read about *that*?

She glanced up at the TV mounted above the seats, almost afraid to look. Phew. Just a piece about a teapot exhibit at the Metropolitan Museum of Art. Cute and wacky teapots. Nothing scary. But then the perky anchorwoman seemed to stare right out of the TV, straight at Abra, when she announced, "Sources in New York City report that media darling and lifestyle expert Abra Holloway has disappeared."

Abra gulped. She looked around. Except for a man with a rolling garbage can headed to clean the ladies' room, there was no one around. No one looking at her or noticing that her face was reflected on the monitor over her head.

"Although she was scheduled to appear on *The Shelby Show* last week as she has every Thursday for the past two years," the anchorwoman continued, "host Shelby Marino revealed that 'Abra Cadabra,' as fans call her, would not be dispensing advice that day. Today, when another Thursday came and went without Holloway, and no explanation was offered for her failure to appear, reporters from several major news outlets began to make efforts to contact her. Shelby Marino and producers on *The Shelby Show* had no comment, but sources close to Holloway have indicated that she has apparently left the show and the city without a trace."

What sources "close to Holloway"? Abra couldn't think of one person besides Shelby she would call remotely close. There was Julian, of course. The world thought he was close, given the carefully crafted image they had portrayed. But Abra knew better.

Breaking into her thoughts, the woman on the television added, "There is no evidence of foul play. In fact, there is very little evidence at all. Her fiancé, millionaire businessman and philanthropist Julian Wheelwright, spoke to the press earlier today."

Abra's heart beat faster, but her eyes were riveted to the TV. Oh, lord, lord, lord. Not Julian. He looked as smoothly handsome as ever, with his blond hair perfectly styled, as always, and his blue eyes so very sincere.

Damn him and his blue eyes both. "Never trust a man with blue eyes," she muttered. She'd had long-term relationships with a total of two men in her entire life, and they'd both had gorgeous blue eyes. They'd also both turned out to be beyond redemption, beneath contempt. *Never trust a man with blue eyes.* She promised to cross-stitch that motto onto a sampler and take it everywhere she went. As soon as she got somewhere she could find cross-stitch supplies and safely sit around and stitch without anyone bothering her.

She felt like bursting into tears. *Oh, jeez.* If brown hair and baseball caps were weird for Abra Holloway, weeping in public was really beyond the pale. She gazed, transfixed, at the TV. She didn't want to see Julian, and yet she couldn't look away. What would he say? Why did he give a press conference? Why couldn't he just keep his damn mouth shut?

"I understand that Abra's many fans are surprised and worried, but there's no need," Julian offered, sending the viewing public a serene smile. "Yes, of course we're still engaged, and no, nothing is wrong."

Nothing wrong? Julian's pants ought to be on fire for that one.

"She simply felt a little stressed," he went on, "a little overwhelmed because of mounting duties on *The Shelby Show* and discussions of her own daily syndicated series. She decided to take a break to get her plans in order."

Her mouth fell open at the boldness of his lies. Still engaged? After she'd thrown his ring at his brilliant, lying white teeth? Stressed and overwhelmed because of *The Shelby Show*? As if. That show was a walk in the park.

And now he was saying that she'd left him a note and told him not to worry, that she loved him and would be back soon. All a pack of lies!

"I know and trust Abra completely," he finished, in a firm and certain tone, "and if she says this is the right thing for her at this moment, then it is. As her fans will tell you, Abra is very focused and she always knows what's right."

Abra didn't know what to think. Well, at least this way maybe no one would be looking for her. Maybe she should be thanking him for trying to take the heat out of her vanishing act.

"He probably just wants to clear himself." She glared at his handsome image. "I hope the police think he murdered me. It would serve him right."

But his face on the screen had been replaced by hers again. She saw footage of herself on *The Shelby*

Show, with her beautifully styled honey-blond hair brushing her shoulders, her skin flawless, her posture perfect. She looked so confident and assured, smiling sympathetically at a guest who wanted help with a husband hooked on outdoor sex. The woman's description of her husband's desire to make love up against the Washington Monument elicited giggles from the audience, but didn't faze the amazingly cool and composed Abra Holloway one bit.

Had that only been a few months ago? Could things possibly have been as simple then as they looked on TV?

"Holloway first came to prominence with her weekly visits to *The Shelby Show,*" the newswoman went on, "as she offered advice and counsel on everything from how to bring order to messy closets to how to acquire better self-esteem and find the love of your life. She acquired the nickname Abra Cadabra because of her apparent magic touch when it came to helping people sort through their problems."

Abra frowned. She hated that nickname. But it only got weirder after that. Someone she had never seen, someone who was identified as her biggest fan, popped up on the TV.

"I am very worried," this stranger confided. "This isn't like the Abra I know. Why would she run away?"

"Who are *you?* You don't know me," Abra argued back at the television.

But the unknown woman wasn't finished. "Abra has always been so together," she said with conviction. "Her life is perfect. Wouldn't she just use the

Ten Steps to Personal Growth, which, you know, she *invented*, to work through whatever it is?"

And then this alleged biggest fan held up a copy of a New York tabloid with the screaming headline Where's Our Abra?

"We need to know she's okay," the woman declared, starting to choke up. "We need our Abra Cadabra to come home, wherever she is, whatever the problem is. Abra, if you're out there listening—please come home. We need you. Please?"

"So there you have it." The polished anchorwoman folded her hands on her desk. "A real mystery surrounding Abra Holloway. The question of the day has become, 'Where's our Abra?' But no one seems to know the answer."

In an airport in Baltimore, Abra Holloway ducked under her baseball cap, picked up her bags and moved farther away from the TV.

1

DETECTIVE SEAN CALHOUN was running late. And if his cell phone didn't stop ringing, he swore he was going to throw the thing in Lake Michigan.

"Damn it." When he pulled it out of his jacket pocket, he saw he'd missed a call, too, somewhere between cleaning the paperwork off his desk and his last meeting with the supervisor of detectives to brief him on a couple of things before Sean left on vacation.

So first he looked at the number from the other call, noted it was his older brother, Jake, the person he was supposed to meet a half hour ago, cursed again, and then answered the new call, only to immediately wish he hadn't.

"Sean, you gotta come over right away," his mother's voice ordered.

"Ma, I don't have time for any more fix-ups, I don't care who they are," he returned.

"You still haven't called my friend Bebe's niece, have you?" she asked smartly. "Or Aunt Ruthie's neighbor, the girl who makes such good meat loaf? She brought Aunt Ruthie cookies yesterday, just to be nice. Can you believe it? Such a sweetheart. She would make a wonderful mother."

Yeah, like that was a real bonus. The last thing he wanted was a wife and kids. He'd been trying to get out from under his family's thumb as long as he could remember. Why create a new generation of Calhouns and prolong the misery?

"Why don't you try Jake?" he suggested, trying not to sound too annoyed, which would only make his mother dig in her heels harder. "He's hitting thirty in a couple of months. I've got a few good years left. So why don't you work on Jake instead of me?"

"Jake, ha!" she said dismissively. "He is so much like your father it's not funny. Why would I waste a good woman on that?"

"Yeah, well, don't waste them on me, either," Sean said flatly. "No fix-ups."

"That's not even why I called in the first place. Sean, you got such a chip on your shoulder, I swear."

"So why did you call?"

"I need you to come over as soon as you can get here," she whispered, hissing into the phone. "I think your father is having an affair."

"Oh, man." This was even worse than another fix-up. "Ma, you know there's no way Dad is having an affair."

Michael Calhoun, one of five deputy superintendents of police for the city of Chicago, was as straight an arrow as they came. An affair? Yeah, right. That would be way too interesting for his by-the-book old man.

"I got evidence," his mother contended.

"Yeah, okay, well, I'm already late to meet Jake," he explained, trying to be patient. This affair thing was a new one for his mother, but not entirely surprising. She had a tendency to be jealous and to keep her husband and her sons, especially Sean, on a short leash. "Jake and I are supposed to pick up Cooper and head to Wisconsin, to the fishing cabin, remember? So it's not a good time."

"Your brothers will just have to wait. This is important."

"Listen, I have a message from Jake here. Let me see what that is and call you right back, okay?" Without giving her a chance to object, he disconnected her and punched in the code to hear his message.

"Something's come up, Sean," Jake's voice growled in his ear. "Sorry. Dad's sending me on this weird errand and I'm not going to make it to Wisconsin. You and Coop go ahead without me, okay? Have a great time."

"Damn it, Jake." Sean clenched his jaw. First Mom and the craziness about Dad having an affair, and now Jake was bailing on him, leaving him with custody of their flaky younger brother Cooper. At times like this, he was really sorry he was a Calhoun.

And his phone was ringing again.

"Sean?" his mother asked. "You didn't call me right back."

"I didn't get a chance."

She made a harrumphing noise. "I'm expecting you within the next ten minutes. Get over here." She hung up on *him* this time.

Funny that Jake had said their dad was sending him on some kind of errand he couldn't get out of. When Dad called, Jake jumped. But when their mother needed something, it was always Sean who got the call, whether he wanted to or not.

His father constantly got on his case about being the family rebel. Some rebel. Hadn't he ended up on the police force like all the rest of them? Wasn't he constantly at his mother's beck and call?

Frowning, wondering if it was too late to become an only child or an orphan, he quickly dialed Cooper, the only member of the family still unaccounted for, but got voice mail. "Hey, Coop, it's Sean. I'm tied up. Jake says he's off on a mission for Dad and Mom is giving me grief about something else. You can go ahead to the cabin if you want, and I'll try to meet you there later."

He dropped his phone in his pocket, shrugged into his jacket, and made tracks to his car. Might as well see what bee Mom had in her bonnet.

He laughed. Dad having an affair. Yeah, right.

"I THOUGHT YOU'D NEVER get here," Yvonne Calhoun declared, swinging open the door before he had an opportunity to knock. He noticed immediately that her face was red, her eye makeup was smudged, and she had chewed off her lipstick, all of which was very unusual.

So she was very upset. It didn't take a detective to figure that out.

"Mom, you okay?"

"Yeah, yeah. Just come in already, will you?"

Sean ducked in the door, feeling eighteen and surly, like he did every time he came back to the Calhoun family house. It was impossible not to revert to a teenage attitude under that roof. *Wipe your feet, say please and thank-you, don't eat or drink in the living room...* Remembering all the rules made him want to do every single thing he wasn't supposed to do.

Jamming his hands into his pockets, Sean ambled into the immaculate living room, avoiding looking at the stern pictures of his mother's parents, Grandma and Grandpa Bergner, on the piano. Next to that were framed pictures of three generations of Calhoun men in their Chicago Police Department uniforms. The True Blue Calhouns. Sean curled his lip. *Yeah. Whatever*.

"Okay," he began. "I'm here now. So what's this junk about Dad having an affair?"

"It's not junk. He is having an affair," his mother said quickly. "Bebe saw him."

"Your friend Bebe saw Dad having an affair?" That was a nasty image. Not that he believed it for a minute. "With who?"

"Well, I don't know who she is. A bimbo." His mom scurried off to the kitchen, but she stopped in the doorway. "Do you want something to drink? A cookie?"

"No, Ma. I want to know what this is all about."

"Sit down. Bebe is here. She'll tell you," she called out from the kitchen. "Bebe, go into the living room and talk to Sean while I get the coffee. And take the pictures with you."

Pictures? Could this get any worse? He had the fleeting thought that maybe it was just pictures of more prospective dates. Maybe this was all subterfuge. But Mom seemed awfully hopped up for just another scheme to marry him off.

"Hiya, Sean," Bebe offered, patting her hair with

one manicured nail as she waltzed into the living room. Bebe was not just his mother's best friend, but also her hairdresser, and her hair had been every color in the rainbow in the short time Sean had known her. Today it was kind of a deep maroon and flipped up on the ends.

"Hi," he returned. "What's this all about?"

"Your mom needs you, honey," she said soothingly. She handed over a stack of photos and then took a seat next to him on the sofa. "I'm real sorry and all, but I saw what I saw. What can I say?"

Sean glanced down at the top picture. "Dad sitting on a park bench wearing a trench coat, with a woman next to him and about three feet in between them. So?"

Bebe tapped the photo with one purple fingernail. "I was at the park, just minding my own business walking my sister's dog—I was dog-sitting, just in case you wondered what I was doing up there, because that is not my part of town—and who do I see but Michael Calhoun, schmoozing with this chickie who is half his age and has a terrible dye job." She rolled her eyes. "The roots!"

"And you just happened to have a camera?"

"No, that was the second time," she told him.

"A second time!" his mother chorused grimly, coming back carrying a mug of coffee and a plate of cookies. "Have a cookie."

"I don't want a cookie. And since when do you let people eat or drink in the living room?"

She waved away his objection. "Everything has fallen apart. Your father is cheating on me. What do I care about a little spill in the living room? Bebe saw the schmuck *twice* with his tootsie. I told you I had evidence." She sat next to him on the couch, pushing him over from the other side, so that he was squashed between the two women.

"Mom, I really think you're making a whole mountain range out of a molehill here," he tried, setting the photos down in his lap. "So he went to the park and some woman sat next to him? So what? Have you found lipstick on his collar? Receipts from crummy motels? Or from jewelry or gifts that weren't for you?"

"No, of course not," she said indignantly. "He's a cop, Sean. How stupid do you think he's going to be?"

"I have no idea. But I'm not willing to make a case of adultery out of a chat on a park bench."

She jumped off the couch and started pacing back and forth. "But he lied to me about where he was. Okay, so Bebe saw him in the park and thought it was odd, just the way he was dressed and the way he was kind of talking to this woman out of the corner of his mouth, all strange."

"I just knew something was weird with him the minute I saw him," Bebe agreed. "It looked very suspicious, you know? So I didn't go over, didn't say hello, nothing, just got the dog and got out of there."

"And she said to me, why was Michael up at Humboldt Park the other day? And I'm wondering about this, because I don't know any reason. The man has a desk job. He doesn't go out in the field anymore. I mean, maybe to a luncheon or something, but the middle of a park? Meeting some young slutty-looking girl? I don't think so." Picking up steam as she continued the story, his mother perched next to him again on the couch, nudging him to look at the photos again. "So I ask him where he was that day, and he shrugs and says he was at work. All day. He remembers because it was such a busy day. And, of course, I know he's lying. So I tell his secretary, who is a doll, to let me know the next time he's out of the office and doesn't have an appointment in the book."

"Oh, Ma..." Sean stared into space. His mother playing amateur detective and checking up on his dad and conspiring with his secretary? And right when the old man was up for a major promotion? He'd never forgive her.

Sean looked up. On the other hand, what *was* Michael Calhoun doing on that park bench with that woman? He narrowed his eyes at the photos. Ever since he'd cracked a couple of hard cases, people had been teasing him about his "uncanny knack for seeing the truth." It was a quote from a newspaper account of his career, and the other detectives—and his brothers—thought it was pretty funny to ride him about it. It was a bunch of baloney, but still... If he stared at the photo of his father and the curvy blonde long enough, would he see the real deal behind this shadowy meeting in the park?

"So the next time your father wasn't where he was supposed to be, I sent Bebe back to Humboldt Park again, you know, disguised, so she could get closer this time. She wore a headscarf and sunglasses and pushed a baby carriage. Your father never suspected a thing," his mom said with fierce satisfaction.

Bebe in disguise, pushing a baby carriage. It might've been funny if it weren't so horrifying. "Let me get this straight. You had Bebe shadowing Dad at the park?"

"So? She got some very good pictures, didn't she?" His mother shook her head. "Same woman, same park bench. Meeting her again. And look at her, Sean. Cheap Christmas trash."

Well, he couldn't disagree. Bebe's clear, sharp photographs showed a dyed-blonde with obvious roots and a frizzy ponytail, big sunglasses, and a dark raincoat over her clothes. She had a good jawline, a determined little chin, and what appeared to be a nicely shaped mouth exaggerated by a load of shiny, dark pink lipstick. The raincoat was open far enough in several of the pictures to reveal a low-cut top, very tight jeans, and the most god-awful pair of shoes he'd ever seen. They were clear plastic sandals with very high heels and glitter and stars plastered all over them. He didn't have to be a detective to recognize hooker shoes when he saw them.

So which was worse? The assumption that his dad was having an affair? Or that he was somehow involved with a prostitute?

"All right," he said grimly. "You've got photos of him with a suspicious woman. Is there more?"

"That's the thing, Sean. I was waiting for him to have, you know, another unexplained absence. But he hasn't. Well, until today, but his secretary heard him on the phone arranging to meet Jake, so I think that was okay."

"Yeah," Sean put in. "I got a message from Jake canceling the fishing trip. He said Dad had an errand for him. So that checks out."

"So since the meeting where Bebe got the pictures, he's been clean. But now…" Her voice was positively triumphant as she made a flourish Bebe's way.

"I saw her again," Bebe whispered.

"At the park?"

"Oh, no. At the airport." Bebe leaned forward, her eyes wide. "I had to go pick up my niece, who is such a nice girl. And so smart. She had a scholarship to Johns Hopkins. You should meet her, Sean. She'd be perfect for you."

"Uh huh. How about the rest of the story?"

"Well, I went to pick up my niece, and who do I see? That same woman from the park! Oh, she was trying to look different all right—her hair was a different color and she had a headscarf, a bandanna kind of thing, but that did not fool me." Bebe, now the queen of scarf disguises, nodded sagely. "I recognized that trick, I'll tell you."

"You saw her at the airport," Sean said patiently. "So she was leaving town. Which is good, right? If Dad was somehow mixed up with this woman, he's not now, because she left town."

"Oh, no, that's the thing," Bebe interrupted. "She wasn't leaving. She was arriving."

"I don't get it. If she was already in Chicago, why was she arriving?"

"We don't get it, either," his mother said, patting his arm. "But that's where you come in."

He had a very bad feeling about this. And since Jake had just canceled out on the fishing trip, Sean didn't really have a good excuse to duck and run, either.

"Sean, my sweet, adorable son," Yvonne Calhoun murmured, putting her head on his shoulder, "we all know you have this..."

He knew what would be next.

"You have an uncanny knack for seeing the truth," she finished. "Sean, you are practically psychic when it comes to these criminals and figuring them out. Disguises, deceptions, it's nothing to you. You just see right through."

Already feeling trapped, he asked, "What do you want me to do?"

His mother sat up straight, laying it out for him without mincing words. "Here's the deal. Bebe saw her at the baggage pickup, she thought it was her so she followed her, she lost her again, but then she picked her out at the Help desk."

"I spotted the headscarf," Bebe said helpfully.

"So she got right in behind her at the Help desk and eavesdropped."

"Wow, Bebe, maybe you should join the force," Sean suggested, trying to keep the edge out of his voice. Keystone Kops on a stakeout.

"I know," Bebe said with a smile. "I was pretty good, I'll tell you."

"And what did you hear when you eavesdropped?" he asked tersely, knowing he didn't really want to know.

"She wanted to know how to get to..."

Sean bent closer, waiting for the word that would come at the end of the dramatic pause. "Where?"

"Champaign," both women said at once.

"Downstate Champaign?" he asked doubtfully. "University of Illinois?"

"Exactly." His mother sat back. "She caught a bus to go downstate to Champaign. So I want you to go there, too, and find this tart and figure out what she wants with your father."

2

As sean unpacked at the Illini Union, he could feel himself begin to relax. A beautiful summer day. A nice hotel room overlooking the Quad on a serene, green college campus where most of the students were gone for the summer. And just about no chance in hell he would ever run into anything remotely connected to the bimbo in the hooker shoes his mother wanted him to find.

Okay, so he felt a little silly being on a wild-goose chase. But as long as he already knew it was a wild-goose chase, what difference did it make? He could hang out in Champaign-Urbana, enjoy himself for a few days, and then head back to town and tell his mother with a crystal-clear conscience that he had done what she'd asked and gee whiz, he just didn't find hide nor hair of the woman she was looking for. Sounded like the easiest case he'd ever been assigned.

And, hey, accepting her crazy mission got him out of town, didn't it? Out of town, away from his desk, away from Mom and her endless string of fix-ups, and away from the responsibility of baby-sitting Cooper at a fishing cabin for a week. Not so bad. Especially when it meant he was back in Champaign-Urbana, which struck him as a great place for a little R&R.

He'd gone to college here, and he had fond memories of pickup basketball games, excellent pizza, lousy beer and general irresponsibility. Good times.

After stowing his belongings, he didn't waste any time, grabbing a bottle of water and quickly taking the stairs down to the ground floor of the Union. He planned to make a fast trip down memory lane to check out some of his old haunts and get his bearings. Then he would tool around town with the blonde's picture, put out a few discreet inquiries, enough to truthfully say he'd done his duty, and get beyond that to the beer and pizza as soon as possible.

First, memory lane. Sean was actually smiling as he slid out the big white doors onto the Quad, feeling footloose and fancy-free for the first time in forever. That smile lasted approximately four minutes, which was as long as it took him to walk down the west side of the Quad, past a group of kids and a guide walking backward on a college orientation tour, and glance up at the auditorium looming ahead.

Because that was when *she* showed up.

Her. As nearly as he could tell, the same one from the photo.

From out of nowhere, she came walking toward him. Automatically, he assessed the details. Head down, looking at the sidewalk. Left hand rammed into the pocket of a long denim coat. Right hand wrapped around the handle of a canvas tote bag with Chicago White Sox written on it.

Her eyes were hidden by dark, impenetrable sunglasses, similar to the ones in the picture. She had brown hair, cut kind of choppy, with the ends visible under a bandanna. Pale skin. Clean, elegant jaw. Feisty little chin. Perfectly formed lips.

Sean blinked. Was he nuts? Or was that really her, the one in Bebe's photographs?

He felt like someone had set off a signal flare inside his head. Surprise, excitement, the thrill of the chase... The zing in the air was as unexpected as it was unwelcome.

Luckily, he had the presence of mind to keep moving after she cut across in front of him and took up residence under a tree. As casually as if he were any old tourist retracing his college memories, he ambled around the steps of the auditorium, turning to gaze back up the Quad, pretending to take in the vista of sun-dappled trees and stately buildings as he gathered data on his mystery woman.

Although she looked a little nervous, fussing with the ends of her hair, arranging her coat, adjusting her sunglasses, she seemed unaware of his scrutiny as she plunked herself down on the grass under a maple tree. Sean bided his time, watching, sipping quietly at his water bottle, wishing his instincts would knock off the high alert already and quit pumping adrenaline through his veins.

Forcing himself to judge the facts, he noted that she wore a lot less makeup than the woman in the picture, plus her hair was a different color and length, and there was no sign of trashy footwear, just plain flat sandals. On the other hand, her lips, face shape, and overall bone structure were a good match, she was the right height, she was wearing a bandanna, which was something Bebe had specifically mentioned, and...

And he had a strong gut feeling, the kind he had learned to trust. After all, an "uncanny knack for seeing the truth" was right there on his resume.

Impatient with that "knack," as always, Sean went back to hard, cold facts. His mantra was that bones didn't lie, and those sure looked like the cheekbones and chin line of the woman in the photo.

What else? He couldn't see much of her body inside the bulky coat, but that itself was suspicious, considering the fact that everyone else around was in shorts and T-shirts or tank tops in the hot weather. Plus she was wearing sunglasses and a scarf and her hair was a phony shade of brown, all of which had "disguise" written all over it. In his opinion, her demeanor was anxious, somewhat furtive, as she huddled there under the tree, deliberately not looking at anyone. She was definitely sending out "pay no attention to me" vibes.

It all added up to someone who had a lot to hide.

But it couldn't be the right woman, could it? Not only had he not expected to find her in the first five minutes he was in town, he hadn't expected to find her at all.

And he hadn't expected her to be so...interesting. Even with the odd clothing, she had this kind of aura, as if she was just more vivid than anybody or anything around her. Call it ESP or just that blasted "uncanny knack" he was supposed to have, but Sean had a strong feeling that if he peeled off the scarf and the sunglasses and the bulky denim coat, he would conclude that she was...

Beautiful. Smart. Intriguing. A knockout.

"Okay, now you're really going around the bend," he said under his breath. Must just be some weird kind of investigative eagerness kicking in, making him feel all hot and bothered in inappropriate ways. It had never happened before, but there was a first time for everything.

Taking a long swig of water to cool his jets, Sean pushed himself back to reality, back to the question at hand. Was she the quarry he was supposed to be looking for?

Physically, the details matched. But the fact remained that she was not at all what he had expected from the woman in Bebe's photo, the one with the frizzy, bleached hair and trashy 'ho shoes. The one who might be playing mattress macarena with his father.

That idea had become even more disgusting now that he'd found her.

Frowning, Sean backed off. Putting a little more distance between them, he looped around the side of the Foreign Language Building to keep an eye on her while he decided what to do. Since he'd had no reasonable expectation of finding her, he had never gotten to the point of planning what he should do if he did. Take a picture and send it back to Bebe for a positive ID? Get fingerprints and try to track down her identity or her rap sheet? Chat her up and see if he could get her to spill what was happening with his father, *if* anything was happening at all? None of it made any sense.

Meanwhile, as he pondered his next move, she still didn't appear to have a clue that he was there, which meant she had lousy survival instincts. Or a trusting nature.

He got his answer on that one when a scruffy kid on a bicycle rode up. "Hey!" the kid shouted, jumping off his bike right next to her. Petty thief? Purse-snatcher? Something worse? Sean decided he was close enough to jump in if his law enforcement skills were required, but he hung back for now. She sat up abruptly, looking very, very nervous, sort of like Bambi in the headlights. But then the kid extended his hand, shuffling his feet, trying to act all tragic and woebegone. Asking for a handout, no doubt. She relaxed, smiling up at him. Great smile. Bright, shiny, sincere. There had been no evidence of that in Bebe's photos, but it was everything you could ask for in a smile.

If he hadn't been such a cynical man, Sean told himself he might've felt all warm and fuzzy after seeing her beaming at the boy.

So she rooted around in a big tote bag, took out a few bucks, and handed them over, after which the boy said thank-you loud enough for the tour group all the way down at the other end of the Quad to hear. Then he leapt back on his bike and zoomed away, leaving Sean to conclude that the girl was either an easy touch or just a sap. Or that had been the best-disguised drug deal in the history of the universe.

Sean cooled his heels, wishing he had a newspaper

or something else to give him a little cover, but it didn't seem to matter, since she didn't look his way. Again, he was struck by her lousy survival skills. He'd been spying on her for a good half hour, and she was clueless.

As he watched and waited, she removed the bandanna, rubbed a hand—left hand, no rings—over her forehead and then carefully tied the scarf back on again; she stared into space; she pulled out a book and dropped it in her lap without opening it; she leaned against the tree and tipped her head back as if she were dozing; she looked a little flushed and clapped her hand over her mouth and left it there for several seconds; she took off her sunglasses and wiped at her eyes with a tissue which he took to mean she either had allergies or she was crying; and she rooted around her bag and took out a package of saltine crackers, which she proceeded to eat, one by one, until she had demolished the whole package. Then she folded her trash back into the bag quite neatly, stood up, hoisted her bag, and began to walk away.

So of course he followed.

Disguise, crying, hungry enough to snarf lots of crackers, possibly a headache or something else physically wrong leading to the flush and the hand over the mouth... What did it all add up to? Sean contemplated some possibilities. Heat stroke from that silly coat? Mental illness but not taking her meds? Undercover or on the lam? Some kind of damsel in distress, emotional or otherwise?

As he trailed her, he found himself with lots more questions, but not getting any closer to answers. If she was the right woman, and the physical resemblance plus how closely she matched Bebe's description made him about eighty percent certain she was, then what had she been doing with his father on that park bench in Chicago, and what was she doing down here now? He was surprised to realize just how much he wanted to solve this riddle. Whether she was or wasn't the "tootsie" his mom wanted him to find, this woman in the long coat and sunglasses, with her crackers and her tissues, she was hiding out in Champaign-Urbana, acting very strangely. And he needed to know why.

Sean stayed about a block behind her as she cut down a quiet campus street and ducked into a coffeehouse. He saw her get a muffin and a carton of milk, slowly consume both at an outdoor table that was remarkably easy to keep under surveillance, and then once again take off walking. It took about ten or eleven blocks of her walking straight ahead, not noticing him skirting around trees behind her, before she walked up to the front door of a small home on a tree-lined side street just off-campus. She put a key in the door and disappeared inside.

No car outside. Nothing in the front yard. No sign that anyone else was in the house.

From the protective cover of a large evergreen outside an apartment building across the street, Sean considered his day's work. Approximately four hours in Champaign-Urbana, and he'd already located his target, shadowed her, and found out where she was staying. Not bad. Not bad at all.

By THE THIRD DAY, Sean had her routine down cold. She would emerge from her house about nine or ten, ridiculously overdressed, carefully buttoned into that damn coat, with sunglasses and some sort of hat. She would walk to the Quad, sit under the same maple tree, eat an amazing number of crackers, stare into space, and look anxious or upset from time to time, with maybe a tear or two. She also fed a squirrel on one occasion, protected herself from an errant Frisbee on another, and twice stopped to read flyers taped to a kiosk.

Nice profile, good nose, excellent smile, beautiful skin. Fondness for American League baseball, given the White Sox bag and the Orioles cap she had on today, and a major taste for saltines, grapes, cheese curls, pizza, McDonald's French fries, muffins, and milk, given what he'd seen her pull out of the tote bag and consume on the Quad. Especially saltines.

Man, he was in bad shape—slipping from surveillance ever closer to plain old stalking—if he was reduced to keeping track of every crumb she ate. At least he had a plan now, and a routine of his own that included a backpack, water bottle, very small camera, newspaper, and a book on college sports, just in case he needed cover if anyone saw him spying. So far, he'd left a few messages for his mother—purposely calling when he knew she wouldn't be in so he didn't have to talk to her—to let her know he was on the case. But other than that, he'd kept quiet about finding his target. Mostly biding his time, he'd managed to snap her picture from various angles to compare to the ones from Bebe, but that was about it. He figured he could watch and wait a little longer, at least until he saw whether she contacted anyone or anyone dropped by to visit her. Like his father.

Even thinking about that made him grind his teeth and think unpleasant thoughts.

"No way that girl is fooling around with my old man," he said grimly from his vantage point behind the front doors of Lincoln Hall. Every instinct he had told him that much, anyway. If she was the one Bebe saw in the park and at the airport, there must be some other reason...

But his analysis of the situation was interrupted when she suddenly bolted up from where she was sitting, abandoning her snacks and her tote bag, careening off toward a secluded area near the English Building and looking a little green around the gills while she did it. Without a second's hesitation, Sean made tracks to follow.

He caught up to her where she'd stopped to hang on to a tree trunk for dear life. She'd knocked off her sunglasses, her hat had fallen off a few feet away, and she was bent over at the waist, with one hand pressed into her stomach and the other firmly over her mouth.

Pale, shaky, unsteady, she turned. Her gaze met Sean's.

Wow. He'd never seen her without the sunglasses. Her eyes were hazel. Even under these circumstances, they were beautiful and warm. Very warm. She paused, blinked, still focused on him, as if she were trying to place him and figure out what he was doing there. He had never felt so awkward and yet so instantly connected to anyone in his life.

Unable to remain merely an onlooker, Sean found himself vaulting into a role as an active participant in this little drama whether he wanted to or not. She was staring at him intently, and he knew he should back off or walk on by before she really did decide he was a stalker. But he couldn't.

Sean edged nearer, picking up the baseball cap. "Sorry," he said quietly. "I don't mean to intrude. But I could tell you were..."

And that was when he finally put two and two together. The bulky clothes, the saltines, the sudden nausea...

She was *pregnant*.

Sean blinked, backing off a step. Pregnant?

Of course. It all made sense. And yet...

The woman who might be his father's girlfriend was pregnant? He felt like he'd been punched in the gut.

3

"Go away," Abra said flatly.

The last thing she needed at this particular moment was some nosy stranger moving in on her and trying to interfere. He didn't look dangerous, just way too cute for his own good, with light brown hair cut short and shoved carelessly to one side, and an intense, serious expression on his very fine face. Wearing a white T-shirt and faded blue jeans, with a backpack slung over one shoulder, he seemed like a regular guy. Or at least an extremely good-looking regular guy. Wide shoulders, nice muscles, lean hips... If he stripped off that shirt, she bet she'd find abs to die for. She had this thing about abs, a thing she had never admitted to anyone, not even herself, really. But she still had it.

She spared him another glance and immediately wished she hadn't. He was adorable, whoever he was, standing there, looking all concerned. And he had blue eyes, too. She might've known. All the worst ones had blue eyes, just to torment her.

"A snoop is still a snoop, no matter how hunky the package," she said under her breath.

He moved closer. "I'm sorry—what did you say?"

Abra groaned, hanging on tight to her friendly tree, wishing her stomach would stop this topsy-turvy stuff. She'd eaten every saltine in sight and she still felt absolutely miserable. But, hey, she was upright. Right now, that amounted to a major victory. Especially with this adorable guy with the fabulous blue eyes staring at her as if she were some exotic wild animal while she tried her darnedest not to barf. If she weren't so sick, she would've considered dying of humiliation.

"I said, go away," she repeated.

But he shook his head, still advancing on her. "I want to help," he said kindly. "For one thing, I think we should get you out of that coat before you pass out from the heat."

Before she could move away, he was right there, gently holding her steady as he unwound her from the heavy denim coat and folded it over his arm. Great. A *chivalrous* snoopy hunk.

"Better?" he asked in that same soothing, annoying tone, laying his palm on her forehead as if she were a three-year-old with a temperature, and she wanted to smack him. Actually, she wanted him to leave that cool hand there forever, or better yet, move it somewhere more fun. But she knew that was just the hormones talking way too loud.

And they needed to shut up. Now.

One hand on her forehead, one momentary physical connection, and all she could think about was how much she liked his long, elegant fingers, how amazing it felt to be touched, what a pretty color his eyes were, how steady his gaze, how hungry she was for a man's hands and lips and...

Shut up. Now! she commanded her noisy hormones.

Still, his fingers felt so good, and those blue eyes, fringed with thick lashes, sparkling with intelligence and concern, were awfully tempting. She could so easily fall into that gaze and never even want to escape.

As a new wave of nausea swamped her, Abra cursed her luck. Just once in her life, it would've been nice to give in and trust somebody to take over, to swoon into his arms and let this sexy stranger carry her off.

Yeah, right. She straightened. Like she wasn't in enough trouble already. All she needed was to add to it by drooling all over a man she didn't even know, someone who could be a publicity hound or a crazed fan or just a garden-variety serial killer.

Starting to panic just a little for a whole new set of reasons, Abra edged away from his hand, mumbling, "Thank you, but..."

But I'm supposed to be in disguise, and now my hat and my sunglasses and even my nice, baggy coat are gone, and all that's left is Abra Holloway, media star, with ugly dyed brown hair and a bad case of the heaves. And even if you aren't a serial killer, you are way too gorgeous to be standing there staring at me while I toss my cookies!

"You still don't look well," he noted. He fished around in his backpack and pulled out a bottle of water. "Maybe you should let me take you somewhere cooler, where you can sit down. In the meantime, how about a drink of water?"

It looked untouched, but still... Did he really think

she would drink out of his bottle? She considered. Well, yes, she would. Her mouth was dry, she was overheated, her stomach was unsettled, and that water sounded pretty good, whether there were Adorable Stranger germs on the bottle or not. Lifting her chin, pulling together every shred of composure she could muster, she found a thin smile for her sweet, misguided Galahad and reached for the water.

After wiping the top, she took two long swallows and then another one, greedily finishing it off. "I feel better now," she whispered, awkwardly handing back the empty plastic bottle. "Thank you."

He smiled. "You're welcome."

Oh, dear. The smile was a killer. Her knees felt all wobbly, and it had nothing to do with the nausea.

Even after the water, she wasn't exactly capable of leaving her handy tree and walking away from him just yet, but she knew she had to get away from that amazing smile and out from under his penetrating gaze. How long before he recognized her, especially with her disguise reduced to a bad dye job and no makeup? She sent him a quick glance. What if he already did recognize her and that was the reason he'd stepped in?

"Thank you so much for your help," she said as steadily as she could manage, stepping gingerly to the other side of the tree, away from Sir Galahad and his helpful hands. "I'm feeling lots better. Really. And I wouldn't want to keep you from whatever it is you were up to when you decided to, you know, leap in and rescue me from my coat. Because I'm fine. Really."

With the tree between them, she tried to laugh, holding out her free hand, signaling to him that he should return her coat. But he didn't.

"I don't think you're fine," he put in. "Actually, I think you should get out of the heat and sit down. In your condition, I mean."

She paused, feeling her turbulent tummy take a dive. "My condition?"

"With the saltines and the nausea, it wasn't hard to figure out," he said softly.

"You're wrong," she rushed to assure him. "I mean, you were right the first time. I was overheated in the coat, that's all. Or maybe it's a touch of summer flu."

"Nice try, but... Listen, this is a little weird, but I noticed you a few days ago and I've been, well, keeping an eye on you." He studied her, wary, alert, way too smart behind those blue eyes. "I think I know who you are and what this is all about."

It took a second for his words to reach her. "You know?" Full-fledged panic thumped under her heart, and she turned her whole body in toward the tree. Too late to hide now, especially since Galahad apparently had X-ray vision.

Oh, lord, lord, lord. Her worst nightmare. Both her worst nightmares. Discovered! Uncovered! Even without the coat, she was so hot she thought she might expire right there in front of him, which would, of course, make it all that much worse because she would be unconscious and unable to defend herself, leaving him free to cart her off to the ER and hit the speed-dial for CNN to tell them that Abra Holloway had just fainted in the middle of Illinois. *Pregnant* Abra Holloway.

Concepts like "CNN," "Abra Holloway" and "pregnant" swirled around her head like bees. And it was all his fault! He was talking again, in that same level, soothing tone, the one that made her think of forest rangers trying to talk wild animals into cages, but she only caught the tail end of it. Not that it mattered. It still didn't make any sense.

"It's understandable," he offered, "that you'd run away and not want to be noticed, I mean, having a baby under these circumstances."

What? What did he know about her circumstances? "Who sent you?" she demanded, moving her hand to her head, refusing to keel over, refusing to fall down and die for one too-smart guy, no matter how spectacular his eyes or his smile. So she went on the offensive while her mind raced with choices. Try to buy him off? Threaten? First she'd better find out what she was dealing with. "Are you a P.I.? Is that it? Did Julian hire you to find me? Or Shelby?"

He narrowed his eyes. "No."

"I didn't think it would be either of them, but... Okay, then, so you're a reporter. *National Enquirer?*"

"No." He just kept staring at her, his gaze rapt and intense, as if he could see right under her clothes, all the way to the soul, as if every secret she'd ever had was easy pickings. He held that gaze—and his silence—till she wanted to throttle him. Or herself.

"Stop staring at me like that. It's unnerving. And if you don't tell me who you are right this minute, I'm going to scream for the cops," she improvised. "You already said you've been stalking me."

"I wasn't stalking you." He brushed that away with one impatient hand, as if the idea of her calling the police was nothing to him. "Listen, my name is Sean Calhoun." He seemed to be watching her even more closely, to see if that name registered. Not as far as she knew. When she didn't react, he said again, "I wasn't stalking you. Just surveilling."

"Surveilling isn't even a word." So he wasn't from Julian or Shelby. Not from the *Enquirer*. Who else could it be? The *Post* wouldn't send a reporter this far, would they? And no reporter worth his salt would use a word like "surveilling."

Sean Calhoun, whoever he was, waited patiently, just watching her, not bothering to argue about the "surveilling" thing.

"Just tell me," she snapped. "Who sent you?"

"Well, if you must know, my mother," he said finally.

Maybe that would've made sense under better circumstances. Did he just say *his mother*? "Are you kidding? Why? Is she a fan?"

"Uh, no. Definitely not," he responded with an edge of sarcasm that didn't add up any more than the rest of it.

What, he was stalking her because she'd given advice his mom didn't like on *The Shelby Show*? "I don't need this right now," she told him, pressing one hand into her tummy and waving the other one at him. "I'm sick as a dog, I don't know who you are, and... And I'm not coping very well!"

"Okay, okay." He advanced on her again, holding up his hands—with her baseball cap in one and her coat draped over the other—as if to show he didn't have a weapon. "I'm not going to hurt you in any way, okay? You need to just calm down."

"I hate it when people tell me to calm down!" Abra returned hotly. "Not that anyone ever needed to before this whole mess, because I was always perfectly calm. Not that they need to now, either, for that matter. It's none of your business whether I'm calm or not!"

After that outburst, which sounded irrational even to her own ears, he muttered an oath, turned away, and then spun back around, his expression dark and brooding. "Look, I just need to know one thing and then I won't bother you anymore. The baby…"

She kept her mouth shut, staring at the ground, refusing to confirm or acknowledge anything.

Finally, he came out with it. "Is it my father's?"

She swung back around to look at him, utterly and completely mystified. His father? She didn't know him or his father. Why on earth would he think her baby had anything to do with his father? "Who is your father?"

"Michael Calhoun."

"But I've never met…"

"Park benches? Chicago?" he prompted.

"No!" she returned quickly. What in the world was this all about? "Me? Park benches? Chicago? No!"

He kept up the interrogation. "Were you at O'Hare a few days ago? Asking about buses to Champaign?"

"Yes, I came though O'Hare. But I don't under—"

Until all at once, gazing at him and his suspicious expression, it sunk in.

He thinks I'm someone else.

Could she be that lucky? Abra scrutinized him, adding up the clues. He didn't appear to be delusional, so the logical conclusion was that it was a simple mistake.

He wanted to know if his father was the father of her baby. And hadn't he said his mother had sent him? Of course she did, if she thought her husband was cheating and making babies. But not with Abra Holloway, because no one would be looking for Abra *here.* With some other woman. So Mom had sent him to find the woman her husband was cheating with, and for some reason, he'd gotten his signals crossed and thought that woman was *her.*

Which meant he had no idea that he'd stumbled over Abra Holloway, missing celebrity. None at all.

Filled with relief and a strange sense of euphoria, Abra began to laugh. Considering the circumstances, it was a little weird to be hooting with laughter, but she couldn't help it. She could tell by Sean's expression that her reaction had taken him by surprise, too.

He thought she was someone else. Phew.

"I'm sorry," she managed, finally getting herself under control. "I'm sorry you're going through whatever it is you're going through with your parents. I'm sure it's not easy being sent to stalk your dad's illicit girlfriend."

"Wait a minute—"

But Abra kept on talking. "You have my sympathies. Really. But I can promise you that I am not in any way involved in your family's domestic drama."

"You're sure?" he persisted. "Because you look like—"

"I don't care who I look like. I'm not her." Now she was starting to get mad. "I've never met you, I've never met your father, and I can't think of even one Calhoun in my acquaintance."

"Maybe he used a different name," he tried.

"Not under any name. It may surprise you, but I do actually know with whom I have been, um, inti-mate." She leaned over far enough to grab her base-ball cap out of his hand and secure it on her head, and then she reached for her coat, but he held it away. "My fiancé is thirty years old and he lives in New York. What are you, twenty-seven, twenty-eight?"

He nodded.

"So even if I did think that Julian had a double life and a secret family in Chicago, which is absurd, he's not old enough to be your father. Satisfied?"

He seemed to consider the issue, which only made her angrier.

"It's not me!" she repeated, more forcefully this time. "And that's far more of my personal business than you need to know."

He didn't say anything, just looked pensive.

"This is insulting," she muttered. "Do I really look like the sort of person who would sleep with a mar-ried man twice her age? And have assignations on park benches? It's so trashy!"

Now that she had worked through panic, relief and hysteria, a new emotion was starting to set in. Ever since she'd figured out she was pregnant, it had been like this, tripping from one emotional quagmire into the next.

So here she was, Abra Holloway, media star, beginning to feel a little aggravated that her gorgeous rescuer, so concerned, holding her coat, feeling her forehead, didn't recognize the real her.

Of course, if he *did* recognize her, it would've been a disaster beyond disasters. But now that he didn't, she was free to feel insulted.

But not insulted enough to stick around long enough for him to figure it out. Collecting herself, she snatched her coat away from him. She couldn't bear to put it back on, but she crumpled it into her arms as she began to look around for her missing sunglasses. "Where are they? My sunglasses fell off when I started to..."

"I think you stepped on them," Sean offered. "They're in three pieces. Over there."

Ah well. It was too late for sunglasses or any other disguise. Sean Calhoun had already seen way too much of her.

"Okay, well, never mind. Thank you for your help. Good luck with your, uh, situation. With your father, I mean." Abra swept away from the tree, past Sean Calhoun, her head held high. But she couldn't help turning back.

"What?" he asked. "What is it?"

She really shouldn't. But she did. Quickly, she offered, "My suggestion is that you open up lines of communication within the family, maybe even go in for family counseling with both your parents. Instead of sneaking around following women you think might be the one, just ask your father if he has a girl-friend. And then take it from there. That's my ad-vice."

He raised an eyebrow. "Thanks. I think," he said after a moment. Was that a smile playing around his lips again?

"You're, uh, welcome," she murmured.

Nice mouth, she noted, letting her eyes linger there longer than she should've. Excellent mouth, actually. It wasn't her fault that it had been way too long since she'd been kissed and she was really hungry for it. It wasn't her fault there were enzymes running through her veins that made her think constantly about hot sex and sweat-slick skin and moist lips and clever hands and strong arms and... Other parts. Was it?

She touched her tongue to her own lip, still gazing at his. His mouth was a bit quirky where it turned up on the edges, with adorable little peaks in the center of his top lip, but with just enough softness to his bot-tom lip to make her think he would be a majorly good kisser.

She shook it off. Why would she think that? He might be a terrible kisser. Just because his lips looked good didn't mean they would feel good or taste good...

Uh-oh. The idea of feeling and tasting his mouth was too overwhelming, too complicated, too alto-gether luscious. As she actually entertained the con-cept of grabbing him and kissing him just to find out, she realized she was feeling disappointed that she might never see him again and never find out if her theory about his kissable mouth was right or not.

Insanity. True insanity.

Grimly pressing her lips together, Abra did her best to damp down her crazy feelings. She spun back around and got away from there—and away from him—before she noticed anything else about him she wanted to touch or feel or taste. Yikes! Hormones were driving her around the bend.

That was her story and she was sticking to it. Blame it all on hormones. It couldn't be that Sean Calhoun was an extraordinarily attractive man and she was feeling vulnerable and needy. Heavens, no. And certainly not that he was exuding sex appeal all over the place from his moody blue eyes and hot body, making her mouth water with the possibilities.

Nope. Just hormones.

She remembered at the last moment to scoop back across the Quad to pick up her tote bag, the scattered cracker packets, and the rumpled copy of *Great Expectations: Managing Your Pregnancy* that she'd ripped the cover off of. It was a miracle her things were still there. But after the day she'd had, she deserved one little miracle.

Were Sean Calhoun's eyes still following her? How long had he been out there, watching her every move? And how could she not have noticed?

She didn't dare look back to where she'd left him. But she could feel him there, still connected to her in some bizarre way, his gaze touching her, his thoughts wrapping around her.

Oh, yeah. Abra shivered. She could definitely feel him. But not enough. Not nearly enough.

As she paused there on the Quad, desperate to run, desperate to stay, all she could think about was all the ways she wanted to *feel* him. His hands and his mouth on her bare skin, her hands and her mouth on his. All of him, hard around her, tangled with her, doing terrible, wicked and exciting things.

Feel him? Oh, yeah. She could really get into that.

4

As he watched her walk away, Sean stayed where he was, juggling a mystifying mix of feelings. First was attraction. Which was really strange. He couldn't remember ever being knocked back by this kind of steamy chemistry the first time he met someone. Especially not a furtive and secretive pregnant woman with a bad attitude and worst case of morning sickness. How could that be attractive? And yet on her it was. Amazingly so.

It was his job to notice things, and he definitely saw the same feelings staring back at him from her eyes. Sparks of excitement and awareness were there every time she glanced at him, in the way her gaze seemed to flicker up and down his body, in the way her pretty pink tongue darted out to moisten her lips.

In short, she kept looking at him like she wanted to eat him up with whipped cream and a cherry on top. And it made him want to find the spoons.

"She's pregnant, you idiot. With someone else's kid. You can't be attracted to her." Frustrated, he swore out loud. He had no clue how to handle that one.

But there was also relief. Yes, he was relieved she'd claimed never to have met his father, and yes, he believed her. He'd spent his adult life judging whether people were telling him the truth, plus there was that "uncanny knack" thing. Both common sense and intuition told him that her panic at having been found out was real, but so was her confusion when he'd mentioned his dad.

If he'd decided once upon a time that he was about eighty percent sure she was the tootsie Bebe had seen in the park, now, after talking to her, he was about ninety percent sure she wasn't.

Okay, so if he analyzed his feelings, he found attraction and he found relief. But there was also frustration, not just the sexual part, but because he couldn't figure her out. At all. And he found himself really, really needing to do just that.

"Thank God she's not messing around with the old man," he said out loud. "But then... Who the heck is she?"

She'd mentioned a fiancé in New York, but she had no rings. And what was she doing in downstate Illinois, pregnant and alone, with nothing better to do than hide behind a terrible disguise as she sat on the Quad and moped? He'd watched her long enough to be sure she wasn't teaching or taking a class or even doing research at the university's famous library. All she did was hang out under trees, eat junk food, stare into space, and go back home. So what did it get her to be in Champaign-Urbana instead of back in New York or wherever she lived? Why the obvious disguise? And why was she giving off sexual energy that knocked his socks off? As well as other, murkier vibes that made him think she was in trouble with a capital T?

"She's got the vibes all right," he muttered, trying to get his mind off the total package of curves and conundrums he found so fascinating. There was just something about this woman, something hungry, something haughty, something...*hot*.

He could feel the heat down to his bones.

She wasn't blatant at all, but there was a major league come-on happening that he wasn't sure she was even aware of. Provocative and innocent, all at the same time. It was a potent package.

Still letting the questions tumble around in his brain, Sean adjusted his position so he could keep her in view. She had the hat back on, but not the coat, and he had to say, now that he had the back view, that he could personally attest to the fact that she provided some very nice scenery. The swing of her hair, the frisky way she walked... And her butt. Sweet. It wasn't polite, but he couldn't take his eyes off that round bottom, temptingly displayed in some kind of shiny grayish pants that were cut just low enough and tight enough to display delicious curves.

She was in a hurry now, bending over to stuff things into her tote bag, offering him an even more tantalizing view. Sean groaned. He had a habit of sitting back, judging, sifting through the facts with all due deliberation, but this was one time he really wanted to just leap into action.

Whatever was going on with her, he liked what he saw. A lot. And every instinct he had was telling him to follow up, press on, keep this connection humming, even if it was strange and weird and convoluted. Let's see, so far, he'd spied on her, practically leered at her, and mistaken her for what his mother had called a "cheap piece of Christmas trash," while she'd made her way through forty-seven packets of saltines and then possibly thrown up on a tree.

He was in the wrong place with the wrong woman; she was pregnant and toting a whole lot of baggage. Not exactly an auspicious beginning.

Thankfully, she didn't stay in that beautiful bottoms-up position long, hustling away from the Quad as if that reporter from the *Enquirer* she was afraid of were nipping at her heels. As she disappeared past the Foreign Language Building, down the campus street that he knew would lead her home, Sean set his jaw. Whoever she was, she was certainly a whole barrel of contradictions.

If her life was such a mess that she needed to sit under a tree and ponder it every day, why did she hand out advice to strangers with such practiced ease? When she'd whipped into guidance-counselor mode, all that Ann Landers-meets-Dr. Phil stuff about the Calhouns going in for family counseling and opening up lines of communication, she'd seemed like a whole different person.

Sean knew very well it was none of his business if an unknown woman with a penchant for advising strangers decided to leave her fiancé and have her baby alone, wherever she chose, in whatever clothing and hair color she chose. But there were so many facets of this mystery he found fascinating. Like Julian, the missing fiancé.

"Julian," Sean said derisively. "Who has a fiancé named Julian?"

But posing that question made him think about its implications. He narrowed his eyes. She had mentioned people named Julian and Shelby, as well as *The National Enquirer*. He was steps away from his hotel and his car. If he wanted to find out who the common denominator was between Julian, Shelby and the *Enquirer*, all he had to do was find the public library and a computer and run a quick Google search. What would it take, three seconds?

Making up his mind, Sean turned in the opposite direction, back toward the Union, keeping his hands in his pockets and his pace steady. No point in hurrying back and calling attention to himself. Julian, Shelby and *The National Enquirer*. Piece of cake. He liked having a path to follow, an investigation to begin. It made him feel a whole lot less unsettled. And he expected to have all the info he needed in no time at all.

SAFELY BACK AT THE sweet little house she was subletting, Abra was stewing. It wasn't as if stewing were a new thing for her, just that she had a new subject to stew about. Instead of angsting over the baby and Julian and her career and where she could possibly go from here, now she was worried about one Sean Calhoun, how much he knew, and when he knew it. And where she could possibly go from here.

"Damn it, anyway," she swore, getting up from the kitchen table to root in the fridge. She was starving again. She had a taste for ice cream, and nothing but Chunky Monkey, with the banana and the chocolate and the walnuts, would do. Of course she had none.

She'd already eaten four pints of the stuff in two days, and she was going to have to make a run to the grocery store for more. But she didn't have a car, so she was limited to what she could carry on foot or on the bus. At the moment, she was going through this particular ice cream faster than she could store it.

"I need Chunky Monkey!" she said angrily, slamming the freezer door, as if yelling and slamming would somehow mysteriously make her ice cream of choice appear. No such luck.

When had her life become so ridiculous? When had she slipped out of control, so that abusing the refrigerator seemed like a reasonable course of action?

"You need to get yourself in gear, girl," she said out loud. "This is just sad. You are Abra Holloway. You tell other people what to do when they can't handle their problems. You are smart, clear-headed, and an excellent problem-solver. It's what you do for a living. You can cope. You have to cope."

After that little pep talk, she closed her eyes and took a deep breath. Exhaling slowly, Abra resolutely resumed her place at the table. She picked up her pen and went back to the list she had been making before the Chunky Monkey panic hit.

Pros and cons: stay or go? was written neatly across the top of the page, with a line drawn down the middle to separate it into two columns. That was as far as she'd gotten.

She chewed on the pen and stared into space. Retreating to this quiet college town for the summer, with so few people around, she'd thought she would be safe. In New York, in Chicago, in L.A., people might notice famous Abra Holloway and ask what was up with her disappearance from the TV show. But in Champaign-Urbana, she'd figured she could find some peace and quiet.

Besides, this was where her life had started to go haywire so many years ago, and she'd had this crazy idea that she could come here and think, just think, about what she should do next, what kind of life she should carve out for her and her baby. As in, retrace her steps, go back to where it started to go wrong, and see if she couldn't make smarter choices this time, to set forth on the rest of her life with a plan and a purpose and a clear sense of direction.

How mature and reasonable and so like the public persona of Abra Holloway, she thought bitterly. How in keeping with the much-vaunted "Ten Steps to Personal Growth."

But now that Sean Calhoun had interrupted... She didn't have the luxury of sitting around reflecting or planning. Even if he didn't know who she was, he'd figure it out soon enough. And no doubt run right to the press.

How much time did she realistically have before the whole world came crashing in on her? How much time before *Fox News* and the *Post* and *Entertainment Tonight* were standing outside the door of her sweet little house, demanding answers?

Where have you been, Abra? Whose baby is it, Abra? How can you, of all people, have an unplanned pregnancy, Abra? Why should anyone respect a word you say when you haven't followed your own advice, Abra?

"I have to get out of here," she said savagely. Standing, she tore off the top sheet from the pad and wadded it into a ball, holding it fast inside her fist.

Once the world knew she was having a baby without a father, that her life was more of a disaster than anyone who asked for her advice, her career would be over. There would be no choice on how to announce the news, how to manage the fallout, how to keep her job as an advice-dispenser when she was a single mother with an ex-fiancé who hated her guts and planned to share that hate with the world if she kept the baby.

"Pregnant, alone, no money and no prospects," she whispered. The worst of all possible worlds.

Making up her mind on the spur of the moment, Abra ran back to the bedroom and pulled all three suitcases out of the closet. She began to grab clothing off the hangers, tossing dresses and shirts carelessly onto the bed.

Time to pack. Time to move on. Again.

SEAN STARED DOWN at the computer screen. "Well, well," he said under his breath. No wonder she'd been so eager to dispense advice. "She's Abra freakin' Holloway."

He didn't watch daytime TV and wasn't much for pop culture in general, so he wasn't surprised not to recognize her. Still, even he had heard the name. She was a bona fide celeb. A hotshot. The kind of woman with fan clubs and endorsements and interviews and press conferences. Not to mention limousines, dinners at the White House, and the cover of *People* magazine.

Gazing back at him from the monitor, cover-girl Abra Holloway looked serene, lovely, elegant, and smart. She had longer, lighter hair that was styled a lot better in the picture than it had been on the Quad, plus she was wearing some kind of expensive, clingy white dress with diamond earrings instead of a bulky coat and a baseball cap. But it was absolutely her. Eyes, lips, nose, even the way she threw her shoulders back and lifted her chin like she could face down anyone and win... Absolutely her.

Just to make sure he wasn't crazy, he pulled out one of Bebe's photos and set it on the desk next to the computer. Glancing back and forth between the photos, he could see now why he'd made the mistake, because there were some similarities in face shape and superficial things like her jawline and cheekbones. But such a difference in level of class. The woman in the photo looked like a hooker, and the one on the screen was a total princess. How could he not have known that at first glance? So much for his uncanny instincts.

"Abra Freakin' Hotshot Holloway," he muttered, unable to take his eyes off her. "Who'd a thunk that?"

Taking his time, Sean methodically browsed through the articles his search had yielded, printing a few good ones, slowly letting it sink in that the woman on the Quad was a celebrity, not at all who he'd thought, and a rare bird indeed. Lots of intriguing info, even if it still didn't add up to enough to satisfy him. And oddly enough, very little about how she got to be the woman with all the answers.

Still under thirty, still single, Abra Holloway has lived all over the country, among many different kinds of people, experiencing jobs in academia, human resources and counseling. In her career as a lifestyle expert, she has helped everyone from tots to senior citizens, from homemakers to tycoons, people hailing from Maine to Hawaii. "Abra has warmth, energy and a real sparkle," raves *People* magazine. "She has that special something that jumps off the screen and into your living room like she's your new best friend." Abra Holloway is here for you, every Thursday on *The Shelby Show*.

That was it. Her whole bio. Even the profile and the cover story in *People* were all about who she was now, not where she came from. It was as if she'd burst onto *The Shelby Show* as one complete counselor package, a real pro who could tell people how to organize their closets or make business meetings more productive or plan amazing family vacations just by clipping coupons, as well as how to get their husbands more interested in sex or win over their mothers-in-law or stop obsessing on their breast size.

But where did she come from? Not a licensed psychologist, it warned repeatedly on *The Shelby Show* Web site. Just everyone's wise sister, aunt, girlfriend, the one who could patiently help you sort things through and come up with the answers that were right for you. She had appeared as if by magic, and her life seemed to be magic, too. No wonder they called her "Abra Cadabra."

Until she suddenly vanished. From what he read in newer stories, it seemed that Ms Holloway had left her perfect fiancé, her cushy job as an expert on absolutely everything, and her wonderful New York lifestyle to disappear off *The Shelby Show* and leave everybody hanging. Fans, media, rivals—everyone wanted to know what had become of her.

"If she had such a perfect life, why did she up and disappear like that?" Sean mused, browsing through the extensive clippings on yet another Abra fan Web site. "And how does the baby figure into all this?"

Did it belong to the smug blond guy with his arm draped around her in several of the photos?

"'Abra at the daytime Emmys, accompanied by fiancé Julian Wheelwright, millionaire business mogul and owner of the company that produces *The Shelby Show*,'" Sean read aloud from under the picture. He sneered at the computer image. "Well, isn't that handy? Her fiancé and her boss, all rolled into one."

He scanned the first paragraph that accompanied the photo. "'Abra is sporting a three-carat pink diamond, a gift from Wheelwright, and she assures fans that she has definitely found the perfect man for her. But no wedding date has been set, and tongues continue to wag that any couple who's been engaged this long will never make it to the altar. Oprah and Steadman have nothing on Abra and Julian.'"

He shook his head. "Good for you for not marrying him, Abra." He could tell from the guy's self-satisfied smirk he was no good for her. So was the baby his? Or was it the fact that it didn't belong to Julian the Jerk that had sent Abra running into the night?

Something had to be wrong with her perfect fairy-tale life with the perfect man or she would've stayed and married him and kept the gravy train going. But he knew from busting enough wealthy guys with major dirty laundry that "perfect" outward appearances could be deceptive. Millionaires and society types could be just as abusive, dishonest and downright creepy as anyone else.

Not that it was any of Sean's business. "Turn off the laptop, walk away, be done with it," he told himself. "Now you know who she is, and that ought to be the end of it."

Shoving his chair away from the computer, Sean ran a careless hand through his hair, feeling downright annoyed. He was a detective, damn it, and a good one. He didn't just start a puzzle and then walk away before it was finished.

It may not have been what he was sent to do, it may not have been smart or even sane, but he felt the need to help Abra Holloway through whatever it was that was making her so unhappy. He wanted answers.

And he knew exactly where to get them.

ABRA WAS DITHERING AGAIN. She hated herself when she dithered. All packed, all ready to go, she was also starving, and she wondered whether she had time to order a pizza before she called a cab to take her to the bus station. She hated to get off-course or to hang around too long, but once she got on the bus out of town, all bets were off foodwise. She might as well stick around long enough to eat here in private rather than out in public at the station.

"Sean Calhoun may have X-ray vision, but he isn't psychic," she grumbled, reaching for the magnet on the fridge with the name and number for the pizza place the previous owner of this house had liked.

No matter how smart, Sean Calhoun could hardly predict that she was going to blow town right this minute. Even if he put two and two together and figured out who she was or called the papers to spill the story, she would already be gone, whether she took the time to order pizza or not.

She dialed Papa Del's and put her order in before she could change her mind again. Decisions were made—leaving in a few hours, hopping the next bus headed out of Champaign, wherever it went, eating pizza in the meantime—and all she had to do was sit and wait.

Quickly bored, she turned on the television. Interestingly enough, she didn't much like TV, even if she herself was on it. Thank goodness it wasn't the right time of day for *The Shelby Show* or she might've felt like another crying jag because she felt terrible about leaving her friend and mentor Shelby in the lurch. As she flipped channels, she resolutely steered away from any news shows which might mention her. That left her a variety of gardening and home decorating programs, talk shows, or reruns of old movies and sitcoms.

It was all depressing, considering she should've been knee-deep in prep for her own show by now. A brand-new, spiffy show, each and every day of the week, with amazingly insightful and interesting guests, where regular old people with problems asked for her advice and she provided answers.

She could've had it all. Fame, fortune, respect, adulation... Not to mention a fabulous designer wardrobe.

Abra shook her head. Wardrobe and adulation were not things she had ever imagined herself wanting. When had she turned into that person, the one who wanted to sit back and bask in the glory of fame and fortune?

"Are you who I really want to be?" she asked out loud, staring at the beautifully dressed, smarmy host babbling on about the glory of sponge painting on the decorating show in front of her. And if so... Why?

"That is not fair," she argued with herself. "I wasn't going to be like her. My advice actually helps people. That's all I wanted. Not the money or the clothes or even the respect. Just to help."

She was thrilled when the doorbell rang, both because she was hungry for that pizza and because it meant she didn't have to look at all the other TV hosts with their silly shows and start these arguments with herself over what might have been, what should have been, what still might be.

"Coming," she called out, looking for her wallet, suddenly off on a new mental tangent. "Hmmmm... Am I going to need more cash before I leave this town?"

Once she was gone, who cared if they spotted her trail and knew she'd used her cash card in Illinois? She would be gone, and that was all that mattered, right? Or would they put a little pin in a map over

Champaign, Illinois, and start plotting routes from there to track her? Abra sighed. This "on the lam" stuff was complicated.

Distracted, she swung open the front door wide, fumbling with a few bills of various denominations. "Was it fourteen or fifteen?" she asked, wondering what you were supposed to tip delivery people in Illinois and if she had any ones in her purse.

"Hi," the man at the door said in a low, vibrant voice that made her toes tingle. "How are you feeling?"

That was no pizza man. Heart pounding, she glanced up.

Sean. Of course. Time seemed to stand still for one dizzying moment. With one whoosh, she felt a rush of joy just to see him again, that big, sizzling zing of attraction and awareness, and a curious need to throw herself into his strong, strong arms and let him decide the wisdom of using ATM's while on the lam. And she felt fear.

"Abra?" he asked softly. "Are you okay?"

With everything else going on in her mind, she wasn't sure she'd heard what she just heard.

"Abra?" he repeated, leaning closer, reaching for her as if he thought she might faint right there in the doorway.

A graceful faint might have come in handy right now. Anything to distract him and give her time to think.

Sean had definitely whispered her name. And she was so busted.

5

"ALL FOR A STUPID PIZZA," Abra muttered. Looking at Sean, hunger still gnawed at her, and it had nothing to do with pizza. Breathing in, she could catch the mix of heat, sunshine and faint summer sweat that clung to him. His presence was tangible, so hard and male and tantalizing. He looked like sex on a stick dangled right in front of her.

She wanted this man. She wanted to grab him by the shirt and lick him all over. Now.

Oh, lord. This was so not the time. And when had she suddenly turned into Slutty McSlut? Her new habit of popping into a state of instant arousal around him was so bizarre, so raw, so unexpected. She'd never experienced anything like this in her entire life. Never with David, the man she'd married briefly when she was young and stupid, certainly never with Julian... Was it just the pregnancy making her drip with need the minute she spotted a full-grown, beautiful man with all the pieces in the right place? Or something else?

Screwing her eyes shut, trying to block her nostrils from inhaling the intoxicating, manly scent of him, Abra lifted a hand to her head, pinching her thumb and forefinger against the bridge of her nose, trying to clear her head. Her life was a huge mess already, without adding the dizzying vapors of uncontrollable lust to the mix.

I have to get rid of him before it gets any worse, she told herself in desperation. But he knows who I am. I can't just kick him out now that he knows!

Besides, he was in. While she was awash in lust vapors, Sean had already eased into her house like the intruder he was, neatly spinning her around and pulling the door shut behind them. How did he maneuver this sort of thing? No muss, no fuss, no hysteria, no need to tackle her or kick down doors or anything but just a little feint to the right, and he was in her house, big as life.

"I didn't invite you in," she pointed out, crossing her arms over her breasts, self-conscious of the fact that they seemed to have swelled recently, and her perky little nipples had decided to make their presence known, too, pushing themselves hard and taut against the thin lace of her suddenly too-small bra. She couldn't breathe, she couldn't think, and it was all his fault.

All he said was, "We need to talk."

"Why? Looking for some more details for the tabloids?" she asked derisively, hoping that acting all mean and self-righteous would cool her sex drive.

With his hands jammed in his pockets, Sean stood very still. There was an economy of motion around him she found very appealing. Too appealing. And the way his hands pulled his jeans tighter across the front... Oh, my, my. Abra, get a grip. And stop staring at his crotch. But he certainly looked well put-together under there.

"If I was going to the tabloids, wouldn't I have done it by now? Wake up, Abra. I'm trying to help." He added, with just a touch of sarcasm, "Because you obviously need it."

She didn't even bother arguing with him. Her brain wasn't working well enough for that at the moment. Thank goodness he took his hands out of his pockets and moved a few feet away.

"I guess you were planning to flee the jurisdiction before I got here, huh?" He was poking around her luggage, haphazardly piled in the living room, showing his disdain with every little curl of his lip.

"So what?" she asked finally. "Did you really think I'd hang around after running into you?"

"But even if I hadn't ID'd you, the fact that you decided to run would've been suspicious." Sean picked up her chocolate brown satchel with its trademark monogram pattern, frowning at it. "Plus these..."

She rolled her eyes. "What the heck is wrong with my bags? Didn't I pack to suit you?"

"I don't know what designer this is," he noted, setting the satchel back down next to the matching duffel. "But it's obviously expensive."

"Louis Vuitton," she put in quietly. "It's French."

"Of course it is. Because you're Abra Freakin' Holloway."

"What's that supposed to mean?"

"It means you are doing a terrible job of staying under the radar," he said darkly. "You have three pieces of matched luggage that probably cost more than the house you're staying in. Don't you think that makes you stand out in a crowd? As soon as you'd blown

town, all I would've had to do was hit the bus and
train stations and ask if the guy at the desk remembers anyone who looks like you. I can see it now. 'Oh,
you mean the luscious babe with the fancy luggage?
Yeah, sure, I remember her. She hopped a bus to Kan-
sas City.'"

Well, when he put it that way, it did sound pretty
dumb. But Abra hid a small smile. Even with her hid-
eous, choppy brown hair, no makeup, skin that could
only be described as a whiter shade of pale, and Sean
thought she was a luscious babe. That was something, wasn't it?

"There's also the fact that you're just not careful,"
he continued, warming up to his argument. "You've
got to be the least savvy person I've ever met when it
comes to lying low. First my mother's crazy friend
Bebe shadowed you all around O'Hare, and now I've
trailed you for four days here in Champaign-Urbana,
and you never noticed any of it."

"You trailed me for four days?" Her mouth
dropped open. "And why was that Bebe person following me at O'Hare?"

"It doesn't matter," he returned impatiently. "The
point is that you don't seem to have the right instincts
for someone who wants to hide out. Plus you drop
way too much information into your conversation,
which is how I figured out who you were. I mean,
you had just met a perfect stranger you thought
might be an investigator or a reporter, and you mentioned both Julian and Shelby. That told me exactly
who you were. A plus B equals Abra Freakin' Holloway."

"Why do you keep calling me that?"

"Because that's who you are," he muttered. "A celebrity. On everybody's hot sheet. Coolest of the cool."

"No, I'm not. I'm just..." What was she, anyway? Did she know any more? *I'm just a regular girl with a baby on the way, no fiancé, no career, and more complications than I know what to do with. Like you.* Aloud, she said, "I'm just a regular girl whose life happens to be a disaster right now."

"I'll buy that." He gave her the full benefit of his gaze again, and she really wished he hadn't. Those blue eyes... But he was taking her to task, so she stopped drooling over him long enough to listen. "You stink at the undercover thing, Abra. You walk around acting all furtive and suspicious, wearing a disguise a kindergartner could pick out, with your dyed hair and your hats and your sunglasses and your big honkin' coat that makes you look like you just came in from the Outback. You might as well carry around a flashing neon sign that reads FUGITIVE."

She lifted her chin, doing her best to glare and not look at him too closely. "So I mentioned Shelby and Julian, and I dressed in a way you found suspicious. And you figured it out. Woo to the hoo for you."

"That's not the point—"

"Let's cut to the chase. You've pointed out all the ways my disguise was deficient. Duly noted. Now what?" Thank goodness her brain was firing on a few cylinders again. "As I see it, you have two choices, Sean. Either you can rat me out to the *Enquirer* and collect a paycheck, or you can do the right thing, leave this house right now, go away, and pretend you never saw me. Well? What will it be?''

No reply. Was he willing to deal? Insulted? Damn the man for being all unreadable and enigmatic. As well as arrogant and pushy and a few other things she was too polite to mention. She added, ''I hope you'll do the right thing, because you seem like an honorable man.''

But what ammunition did she have to use to persuade him? Sex? Abra tried not to blush as she momentarily—crazily—considered offering a quick roll in the sheets to keep him quiet. Other women traded sex for secrets. Why couldn't she? Her body, so hungry to seduce this man, hummed with the very idea. But she knew who would be most eager for that arrangement. Her, now that she was Princess Horny of Lower Horndovia. Except in her current state, she'd probably beg him for another tumble as soon as they were done. And then another and another...

Every tabloid on three continents would be lined up outside while she begged Sean for one more trip on the merry-go-round. *Why, Abra, maybe Julian is right... Maybe you would sleep with anything that moved...*

Terrible, terrible idea. She mumbled, ''I—I could pay you, you know, to keep my secret.''

He shook his head. ''Let me guess. You want to write me a check with your autograph on it that I can take right to the papers to *prove* it was you, just in case somebody doesn't believe me. Look here, world! I've got Abra Holloway's autograph!''

Okay, bad idea. "No, of course not. I mean, maybe. But I do have some cash," she put in hastily. "I brought a lot with me, but I'm down some, since I paid for my summer sublet in cash. But I can get more with my ATM card. I was thinking about that, anyway, because after all, I'm leaving town, so I can use my card before I go, right? I'll get you however much you want, and then I'll just get on the next bus like I was planning, and that will be the end of it."

"No, I don't want your money, and no, you shouldn't be using your ATM card. And no, you shouldn't hop the next bus. I thought you were supposed to be smart." He advanced on her, looking all intent and sincere. "Abra, if people from the tabloids are trying to find you, using your ATM card is like sending up a signal flare. And buses and trains in the general vicinity of the ATM are the first place they'll look."

He didn't need to be so high-handed about it. Stung, she demanded, "But what is the right thing, then, if everything I think of is wrong?" She didn't get time to hear the answer. The doorbell rang. Exasperated, she turned to him. "Who can that be? Did you tell anyone I was here?"

His voice and his expression were dry when he said, "I'm guessing it's your pizza."

She relaxed a little. "Oh. With all this other stuff going on, I forgot about that. Thank goodness. Just my pizza." Moving toward the door, she glanced around for the money and purse she'd dropped somewhere when Sean came in. "Do you see my purse?"

"Better let me," he interrupted, cutting in front of her. "Just in case it's not the pizza. You haven't had any other encounters around town with people who may've recognized you, have you? Besides me, I mean?"

"No. Not that I know of."

"Yeah, I'm sure you're right." He smiled again, that small, crooked one that made her toes tingle. "If there were anyone on your trail, I probably would've spotted them while I was watching you."

She couldn't get over the fact that he had been watching her—for four days?—and she didn't notice. Maybe he was right. Maybe she was a pathetic excuse for a fugitive. The thought rankled. No one had ever asked for her advice on how to run away, how to go underground, how to blend in, but she felt sure she could've researched it and given wise counsel if she needed to. So why was she so bad at it herself?

Those who can do, *and those who can't give advice on television.* It was annoying.

The doorbell rang again, more insistent this time, and Abra grabbed her purse. "Look, it's definitely the pizza. I can see his car out the front window," she argued. "It's my pizza. I'm paying."

"And what if the delivery guy is a fan of *The Shelby Show*? Or someone with a subscription to *People* who saw you on the cover?"

"Even if he is, he wouldn't recognize me," she tried, but she knew very well he just might. Especially since she'd lost her sunglasses and hadn't thought to wear the coat or any protective head covering just to answer the door. Giving in, she pushed money into Sean's hands. "Okay, you win."

With the door open the barest crack, it took Sean about three seconds to dispatch the delivery boy while she hovered inside. She could smell the pizza already, and her stomach rumbled loudly in anticipation. As soon as Sean turned around, she descended upon him and grabbed the hot box out of his hands.

"I guess you were hungry," he noted coolly, trailing her into the kitchen. "You ordered all that just for you?"

Already digging in, Abra belatedly found paper plates and tossed them on the kitchen table next to the open cardboard box. "I was starving," she explained, taking a chair at the table. "There are napkins here, and I set out a plate for you. So feel free to jump in."

"No way I'm getting between you and that pizza. I might get chewed up and spit out before you realized I wasn't part of the meal."

If he were part of the meal, she had the feeling she wouldn't need to sublimate by wolfing down pizza. "Very funny," she said defensively. "So sue me for being enthusiastic when I'm hungry. I'm having a hard time controlling my appetites right now."

"Oh, really?"

She wished she'd chosen a different word than "appetites."

Trying to get herself back to the topic of food with no treacherous tangents, she murmured, "This is really yummy," already devouring another square, dripping with cheese and studded with spicy sausage. Chewy, cheesy, just enough crust... It did taste fabulous.

"Yeah," he said doubtfully, his gaze lingering on her mouth. "You're making it look, um, yummy. But still, is pizza really what you should be eating right now?"

"I don't know." She took another big bite, closing her eyes and concentrating on the cheesy goodness. "Is there something wrong with pizza?"

"Shouldn't you find out?"

Was he pushy or what? "Look, I have a book about the right diet for the mother-to-be, okay? I got to the part about saltines for morning sickness, and I tried that, didn't I? Didn't really work, either. So you'll forgive me if I just haven't managed to read the rest of it yet."

Whoa. That sounded terrible, like some reckless, stubborn guest on *The Shelby Show*, the kind who came to Abra wallowing in denial, daring to be set right. Which Abra was happy to do. Once again, she was struck by her own double standards, and she didn't like it one bit. Being stuck in a limbo of bad choices and bad attitude was not how she saw herself.

She could see Sean was opening his mouth, ready to chastise her yet again, and she just couldn't handle it. Holding up her hand, complete with slice of pizza, she stopped him before he started. "I'm under a lot of stress, which I did read far enough into the book to know isn't good for my baby. You second-guessing every detail of my life isn't helping. I don't want you to lecture me, okay? I just want you..."

Feeling a flush of hot color stain her cheeks, Abra broke off in midthought. What did she "just want"? How about for Sean to peel off her clothes and throw her across the kitchen table for mad, passionate sex, right there, right then, and take both their minds off all her problems? Sean without a shirt, pushing off his jeans, dispensing with preliminaries, as eager as she was to get to the main course... Talk about avoidance therapy. She just about choked on a piece of sausage.

He didn't seem to know what she was thinking, thank goodness, as he retreated a step, pensively pacing around her kitchen. Her mouth was dry and the pizza didn't taste as good anymore, but she forced herself to bite and chew.

"Look, Abra," he said after a long moment. "I won't give you away or make things any more stressful for you. I didn't mean to sound like I was lecturing. But you really do need to do things differently if you're going to stay undercover. You do realize that, right? Or somebody else will recognize you just like I did."

"Whatever," she said with a sigh, unable to process what it was he was saying. Her mind was still back on imaginary kitchen-table sex, especially the part where he stripped off his jeans and covered her naked body with his. Sean, naked. Lord, lord, lord. That ought to be illegal, even for a fantasy. She shook her head, trying desperately to clear her mind. "Maybe."

Sean pulled a chair up at the table, close enough to make her nervous. She ran her fingers over the wooden edge of the table, back and forth. Would you get splinters if you really did take a ride on the kitchen table?

Narrowing his gaze, Sean asked softly, "Can you tell me why you ran? Maybe I can help if I know why."

That wasn't what she wanted to be thinking about right now. He wanted to know why she was on the run? Why so concerned? Why so deadly serious? "Isn't it obvious?"

"Not really."

His speculative gaze lingered on her face. She swallowed. "I'm Miss Know-It-All on television. I'm pregnant. I'm not married. Isn't that enough?"

"You also appear to have a fiancé you've had for some time and a job and friends and a strong support system. All kinds of things that should've been hard to leave behind."

"I suppose. But Julian and I..." She trailed off.

With her mind still spinning on erotic images of Sean, her relationship with Julian was *so* not something she wanted to talk about. Wasn't Sean the one who had warned her about giving away too much information in her conversation with strangers? She still had no reason to trust him, and the fact that she was aware lust was clouding her judgment should be making her shut up even tighter. Besides, who could look at Sean, with his true blue eyes, all sincere and stalwart, and want to spare one thought for Julian the slime bucket, the one who'd sworn the baby wasn't his and threatened to smear her name all over the media as a cheap trick who slept around, even though he knew good and well she didn't? Good ol' Julian.

I never wanted to be a father, Abra, and you knew that. I'll fight you tooth and nail if you try to pass off that kid as mine.

It was ugly and humiliating, and explaining it to Sean wasn't even a possibility.

How funny. She hadn't realized it before. Julian had been wronger than wrong when he'd called her a slut, but now, with her crazy hunger to jump on Sean Calhoun right there in the kitchen, it had turned out she was edging closer to Julian's trampy image with every wayward erotic fantasy.

"What about Julian and you?" Sean persisted.

Cautiously, she went on. "Julian and I were clear on where we were headed. I knew that going in. So I shouldn't have expected more when, um, complications arose."

"Okay." Sean's gaze grew even more probing. "I'm not sure what that means. Are you saying he is or isn't the father?" He waited, but she didn't say anything. "Whoever the father is, don't you think he deserves to know you're pregnant?"

"He knows." Pushing away from the table, Abra stood abruptly, crossing to the fridge to get herself something to drink. Something cold—like ice water poured over her head—sounded good. "He made it clear he won't be...helping. Or anything else. Let's just say this is not something he wants."

"And that would be Julian?"

This time she was resolute. Her lips were sealed.

"Okay," Sean said again. She could feel his eyes on

her, even with her back turned. "You're sure you're alone on this, and you think your public wouldn't understand Abra the single mother? Have I got that right?"

"I was between a rock and a hard place. That's all I'm saying."

After a pause, he asked, "So you're on the lam, just the kid herself, not reading the books, not taking the vitamins, eating junk, and basically not taking care of yourself?"

"Such flattery," she remarked. She swung back around to face him, water bottle in hand. "You said you wanted to help. How do you propose to do that, Sean?" she ventured. "By turning me in? Calling Julian to tell him to step up? What?"

"None of the above." He set his jaw in a hard line, as if he weren't brooking any arguments. "I'm thinking I should stick around."

"Oh, no, you're not. You're absolutely, positively not."

Shaking her head, starting to panic a little under the influence of way too many cravings toppling over each other, Abra took a step backward, tripping over a small stool that was there to help her get into the top of the kitchen cabinets. She could feel herself flailing to hang on to her balance. But faster than a speeding bullet, Sean was behind her, holding her steady.

Her breath caught in her throat and she pretended it was all to do with almost falling down. But it wasn't. Was it so wrong to enjoy the feel of his warm hands on her shoulders, to lean back into his hard, strong body just a little, to take a nice, deep breath and drink in his sunny smell?

"This is why you need me," he murmured. "I'm definitely staying."

6

"YOU NEED SOMEONE TO catch you when you fall."

For about half a minute, it seemed as if she might actually be receptive. She whispered something like, "This is a really bad idea," but the fact that she let herself sort of drift back into his chest said the opposite.

But then she practically leapt away from him, spinning around and raising her hands as if to hold him off. "Oh, no, you don't!" she declared, backing up toward the table.

"Abra, stop. You could trip again and—"

"I'm not tripping," she cut in. "And you're not staying."

"But I told you, I can help you."

"Right. Help. Uh-huh." She started jamming leftovers into the box, slamming the lid closed on half a pizza. "Just how stupid do you think I am? You already admitted you've been stalking me, and you had some cockamamie story about your mother sending you after your father and his girlfriend, but you dropped that one pretty fast, didn't you?"

"Look, that was true. I wasn't stalking you. My mother really did send me." He realized this was all quite unusual, but it made perfect sense to him. Well, not perfect sense. Even he couldn't figure out why he was so drawn to her or why he was pushing himself into her life. "It's just... I come from a family like that. Big on duty and responsibility, you know?"

It was sort of like his dad stopping to help an elderly lady with a flat tire, or his brother getting the neighbor's cat out of a tree. *You just can't see a problem without wanting to fix it,* his mother had complained to his dad on more than one occasion, *whether it's your problem or not.* It was why people called them the True Blue Calhouns. They were rescuers. They stood up when it was time to be counted. They did what needed to be done.

Sean had never been all that clear that he fit under the True Blue umbrella—he had certainly fought against it long enough—but it looked like when push came to shove, or when a beautiful, crazy damsel in distress showed up—he was as True Blue as any of them. He just couldn't help himself.

But she wasn't listening. She was too busy assassinating the pizza box, trying to smash it sideways into a kitchen trash can that was too narrow.

"Give me that," he told her, moving to take it away from her. But she held up the bent cardboard like a weapon.

"Stay away from me," she ordered. Her words began to trip over each other as she brandished the pizza box at him. "I don't know you. I don't have any reason to trust you. While I admit there's a certain attraction, that is not my fault. It's all about hormones. And wanting to have hot sex on the kitchen table is not enough of a reason to invite someone in for the duration. In fact, just the opposite. That's a very good reason to make someone leave right now so it never becomes an issue!''

His jaw dropped. Hot sex on the kitchen table? Where in the hell did that come from? He was not a man who was easily surprised, but that blindsided him like a two-by-four to the head.

He glanced at the table and then back at Abra. He could see the precise moment her brain caught up with her words, as absolute horror filled her wide eyes. The battered pizza box slid from her hands, clattering to the floor unnoticed. Sean quickly decided that ignoring the whole ''hot sex on the kitchen table'' thing was the better part of valor, but he couldn't help storing away the mental image for later enjoyment. Yikes. Abra Holloway was one interesting woman. He could be up for hot sex on the kitchen table with her anytime.

''Abra,'' he tried again, as calmly as he could manage, ''I'm not a stalker.''

''I don't trust you,'' she repeated. ''This whole thing is just too weird. And there are a lot of people in this world who want to be best pals with Abra Holloway, you know. Not me, but *her*. The television version. Abra Cadabra,'' she said with a sneer.

''I've never seen your TV show. I'm not some crazy fan.''

''Yes, but how do I know that?'' she demanded. ''With all these people, it's all about being next to the star, starting a fan club, building a Web site, being my date at the Emmys, you know? It's freaky when you're used to just being a regular person, and suddenly you have to wonder whether every person you meet wants to know you for you, or just for the celebrity rub-off." She paused. "I don't think that's you. But I'm just not sure."

Feeling impatient and annoyed, Sean shoved a hand through the short strands of his hair. "You know, *I* should be the suspicious one," he said sarcastically. "You have a lot to lose here if I decide to spill the beans. If you were really into keeping me quiet at any cost, you might just be seducing me into being your patsy, your co-conspirator, your mark. The star takes advantage of Joe Schmoe from the sticks. Maybe you're really clever, and this is all a scam."

He was kidding when he started that thought, but now he wasn't so sure. He paused, thinking about the hot light in her eyes, the signals she was sending, and even the way she'd let that kitchen-table thing slide into the conversation. Was she a lot less innocent than she seemed? Had she planned all along to reel him in and string him along?

"Seduce you into being my patsy?" she repeated in a squeaky voice. He could see the spots of color on her cheeks as she cleared her throat. "Like some femme fatale? I would never... I could never do that."

But she had considered it. Guilt was written all over her face. Sean couldn't quite believe it himself, but there it was. It had clearly crossed her mind to offer him sex for silence, either to bamboozle him long enough for her to skip town, or just to seduce him into cooperating.

Damn. He might've gone for it if he'd known. What had she called it? Celebrity rub-off? The idea of "celebrity rub-off" had some interesting implications if Abra was the one doing the rubbing.

Nah, he wouldn't have taken her up on that offer. But it might've been fun to ponder. He spared her another glance. Abra just kept surprising him.

"I would never have done that, Sean," she repeated.

"I know." And he did. Instinctively, he knew that she might've let it flit through her mind, but she was simply not a good enough liar to play the use-and-discard game. Resolute, he got back to the issue at hand. "If you were really a femme fatale, you'd be better at hiding out than you are." He shook his head. "You've been making some basic mistakes, Abra. It just so happens that I know more than you do about how to successfully evade detection, how to hide in plain sight, how to go undercover."

"Why is that?" she asked in a more composed voice. The blush was still in her cheeks, but he could tell she was trying to hold herself together and not make any more major gaffes like the kitchen-table one. "Who are you, Sean? Why would you know about that?"

"I'm a cop. A detective with the Chicago Police Department." He pulled his shield out of his pocket and flipped it open so she could see. "I have ID if you want to see it."

"Oh, my God." She pushed past him, barely glancing at his badge, as she sank into a chair. "No wonder you used *surveilling* as a verb. I should've known."

"Huh?"

But she wasn't listening. "I'm unlucky enough to

look like somebody's dad's girlfriend just when I don't want anyone looking for me, and the somebody turns out to be a Chicago cop. I'm dancing around the edges of propositioning a cop. Oh, my God."

Did she say *propositioning?* Did he miss that? "What do you think I'm going to do, arrest you?" He shook his head. "Have you committed any crimes? Maybe a bank robbery before you left New York? Or did you smack Julian the Jerk upside the head with a nightstick?"

"Heavens, no, but..." Her eyes met his, and her expression held a certain amount of skepticism. "You're really a detective, and yet this is the best use of your time, following me around? Don't you have any cases or suspects or criminals to apprehend or anything?"

"It's a long story."

"Try me."

She just kept staring at him, her gaze level, all demure and composed, her hands folded on the table, like she thought she was at Sunday School. After a moment, when it became clear she wasn't going anywhere until she got what she wanted to know, he figured he might as well tell her. He knew who she was; maybe it was time he returned the favor. "If you really want to hear the whole thing..."

"I do."

"Okay. So I'm on vacation." Settling himself against the counter, Sean swung open a cabinet door, felt around for a glass, and started to run the faucet to get cold water, all without taking his eyes off Abra. "For this vacation, I was supposed to meet my brothers—I have two, both cops—it's like the family business. We were supposed to meet in Wisconsin for a fishing trip. Two weeks. But Jake, my older brother, canceled at the last minute. And my mom nabbed me. She thinks my father is having an affair. Which is ridiculous. You have never met a straighter arrow than my father."

Looking very serious, Abra nodded, chewing her lip, letting him know she was following so far. Her gaze seemed to zigzag between the cabinet and his hand holding the cup, and Sean found himself wondering, for just a second, if she had any fantasies about kitchen sinks or counters or even refrigerators, or if it was just tables. Okay, best not to go there.

With difficulty, he pulled himself back on track. "So, we've got my dad, unlikely to be pursuing extramarital options, and on the other side, my ma, who is just sure he is."

The water was cold enough to suit him now, so he filled his glass and took a swallow before he went on. Lord knew he needed to cool off a few degrees. He went back to his family. That was always a real chill pill.

"My mother can be kind of crazy, by the way. Not bad crazy. Just mixed-up, obstinate crazy. Hard to get around when she has her mind made up," he explained. "So she and her friend Bebe, the one I told you who picked up your trail at O'Hare, cooked up this nutty idea that my dad was fooling around, and they even took pictures of him meeting with the alleged love interest on a park bench, which they showed me."

"And this park-bench person looks like me?"

"Kind of. Not really. She's sort of, well, trashy. But the jaw and the nose are similar, even the lips, and she had sunglasses and a raincoat and a scarf, just like you. It was enough for Bebe, who was playing Nancy Drew. Bebe heard you tell somebody at the airport that you needed a bus to Champaign, so she hot-footed it back to my mother, who called me and ordered me to go find you." He lifted his shoulders in a brief shrug. "Wrong woman, wrong place. If it hadn't been for the scarf and the sunglasses, I don't think Bebe would've looked at you twice."

Abra blinked, as if she were confused. "Okay. I guess. But that still doesn't answer why you agreed to be part of it."

"Because I didn't think there was a chance in hell of ever finding the person they wanted," he confessed. "I thought it was a wild-goose chase, but it would give me a chance to get out of town, come back to U of I, have a few beers and some pizza, see some old haunts. No harm, no foul."

"You went to school here?" she asked suddenly, leaning forward. "So did I. I wonder if we were here around the same time. Well, I only stayed two years. Then I dropped out because..." There was a long pause, enough to clue him in that there was definitely a dropout story he wanted to hear. "Never mind."

He nodded. He could bide his time. For someone who was trying to hide, she really wasn't very good at keeping secrets. So she went to this university and dropped out, and there was a story there. He filed the bit of information away for future reference.

"So that's it," he finished up. "My whole story. I

saw you, you fit the description, and I kept an eye on you to see if you were in contact with anyone useful. Like my father."

"You could've saved everyone a lot of time by just asking your father instead of coming chasing after me," she noted.

"If you knew him, you wouldn't say that."

"Oh, yes, I would." As if she had repeated these same words a hundred times, she declared, "It's always better to face these things head-on, to talk it through and work it out. Suffering in silence isn't good for anyone, especially when a few simple questions can erase a world of misunderstandings."

Sean raised an eyebrow. "I'll keep that in mind. And is that what you're doing, facing things head-on?"

"I..." But she pressed her lips together. "This isn't about me. It's about some other, trashier person who apparently vaguely resembles me. Speaking of which, when exactly did you decide I was not the right person?"

"Today. It became clear today that you couldn't be the woman from the park bench." He shrugged. "Since I never really cared about finding her in the first place and it was more of an excuse to get out of town for some R&R than anything else, I didn't mind blowing off that wild-goose chase."

"And then?"

Reluctantly, he answered. "And then, watching you, I got curious. I wanted to know who you were and what this was all about."

"Curious. Hmm." Abra nodded, looking very pensive. "Kind of an occupational hazard, right, Detective Calhoun? You see a mystery and you want to solve it. You see a damsel in distress and you want to solve all her problems."

"Kind of. I guess." Considering he had called her a "damsel in distress" himself, he could hardly disagree.

"And where does this lead us, Detective? You take me on as a pity project while you're on vacation. And then what?" Her tone sharpened as she scooted to the front edge of her chair, tipping her head up to skewer him with her amber gaze. "You get a new merit badge, I get clued in on how to pass with the smarter class of fugitive, and we go our merry ways?"

Sean smiled. She certainly had a way with words when she got wound up. "Listen, Abra, I can tell you don't like being the damsel in distress. You seem a lot better equipped to be Miss Large-and-in-Charge. But just this once, you're stuck on the receiving end." He paused. "How long are you planning to be on the run?"

"I—I don't know. Just long enough to decide where to go from here." Her hazel eyes were wide and vulnerable. "About the baby, the career, the..."

"Fiancé?" he supplied.

"No. That was decided. Dead. Done."

He nodded. "Okay. First rule for fugitives—get yourself someone on the outside who can provide money and cars and places to stay. For you, right now, that would be me."

"Money and cars and places to stay?" she asked doubtfully.

"Uh-huh," he said serenely. "If you let me help you, I can be the one who opens the door and pays the pizza guy, the one who loans you a car, transfers money from your account to Bermuda and Switzerland and back so you can use it without the *National Enquirer* picking up where it's going, and generally makes it easy for you to lie low as long as you want, wherever you want."

He could see her eyes light up as she began to consider the possibilities. So he pressed home his advantage. "Or would you rather go on the run again, without the right preparation, dropping clues all over the place, wandering into another town, where you have to try to play hide-and-seek with another set of strangers who may or may not recognize you? I can help you put together a decent plan. Or I can leave you to your own devices. It's up to you."

"It would be really nice not to be so alone, but—but I still don't see what you get out of this." Abruptly rising from the table, she crossed to him, snatched the glass out of his hand, and set it by the sink. She opened the fridge and handed him a bottle of water. "Drink this. I don't trust the tap water here."

"Right. But you trust the pizza." His smile widened. "You know, I like you. I'm not sure why myself. Princesses are not my style. Especially media princesses with designer water and designer luggage and big, fat designer chips on their shoulders. But you're smart and you're funny." He didn't mention the incredibly sexy part, even though it was never far from his mind. "I do like you, Abra."

"Fine. You like me." She stood her ground, right in

front of him, challenging him, gazing up into his eyes, just inches away, close enough that he could smell her shampoo. It was something fruity. Something nice. "I hate to tell you this, Sean, but everybody likes me. It's part of the carefully constructed media package. So, you liking me, is that your whole motivation?"

"Maybe your undying gratitude. Or a book deal and a visit to *The Shelby Show* when it's all over," he said with a sardonic edge. But his mind was elsewhere. He'd been thinking about how shiny and soft her hair was, wondering what it would feel like between his fingers, and he'd lost track of his argument. "Bottom line—you need me, Abra."

As she considered, she lifted her pointy little chin, looking all saucy and feisty and making him want to kiss her. Bad. Maybe even check out that kitchen table she was so fond of. Worse.

"I guess so," she allowed.

"And you'll unpack and stay and let me help you?"

"Maybe."

"You're a hard case."

"I try." And then Abra laughed, and he was a goner. Her smile was a knockout, but her laugh hit him where he lived. "I know a good deal when I see one," she noted. "You're smart, you're honest, you're very, very cute, and you obviously know this fugitive thing backward and forward. I'd be crazy to turn down an offer like that."

"Not just cute, but very, very cute?" he asked, amused.

She licked her lip. "Yeah."

"So don't turn down my offer."

"Don't press your luck." She extended her hand, as if to shake on the deal. Sean took her hand, but he didn't shake it. Instead, he reeled her in, held her fast, and lowered his mouth to hers.

He'd been wanting to kiss her since the first moment he saw her. He wasn't going to miss his chance.

"Ohh." She made a nice little whimper, mixing surprise and eagerness, and he nibbled her bottom lip, planning to take it slow. One little kiss. Totally casual. What was the harm?

But her arms wound around his neck, her mouth was wet and hot and opening for him, and he found himself pulling her tighter, slanting to deepen the kiss, recklessly diving in. God, she was radiating heat. It was as if someone had flipped her switch directly to "high" without trying any of the lower settings.

Her breasts grazed his chest, and when she rubbed back and forth a little with the kiss, her moans got louder, sending him higher, faster, harder. She seemed to be melting into a puddle of need, wrapping around him, urging him on, even sliding one hand under his T-shirt and feeling him skin to skin, while he was fighting to stay in control. And losing.

"Perfect," she breathed into his mouth, dipping her fingers around the curved muscles of his abs. "I knew they'd be perfect."

The sensation of her greedy fingers skating across his fevered skin was unbelievable. He slid his palm over the curve of her bottom, settling her in closer, right up against the heavy ache of his desire. "Abra," he whispered, bending to press his lips into the soft nape of her neck. "Don't stop."

But something changed and she did just that, going rigid in his arms.

Inhaling sharply, she unexpectedly yanked her hands away, backpedaling so fast he thought she might fall over. He reached for her, unwilling to let her fall, but she slapped him away. "Sorry. I'm so sorry. But, Sean, look, this can't happen."

He wanted to tell her that he was just going for a simple little kiss and she was the one who turned it into something entirely different, something incredible and amazing and over the top, but he didn't think that would go over too well right now.

"We can't let that happen again," she said plaintively. "It was not part of the bargain. You're supposed to be helping, not making things worse."

"I didn't do this all by myself." He swore under his breath, turning to the refrigerator, opening the freezer door, letting icy air blast him in the face. "I wasn't the one who brought up hot sex on the kitchen table. And I sure wasn't the one shoving her hands under my shirt."

"I said I was sorry."

"So you did. So you did." He slammed shut the freezer door, leaning his forehead against the cool surface. He felt like knocking his head a few times for good measure, but he refrained.

"I am very attracted to you." Her words came out slow, measured, and a little grim. "I'm sorry. There are so many new feelings flooding me right now. But

I can't put you and...this...into the middle of that. You have to understand, this is kind of how I got into this mess in the first place."

Of course it was. How stupid of him. Sex and passion had put her right here. After seeing the guy's picture and hearing Abra's tone when she discussed him, he doubted that passion was for Julian the Jerk, but it hardly made any difference. And her story was becoming clearer, if he was putting the pieces together properly. In the name of irresistible passion, she must've cheated on her oily fiancé, who'd promptly dumped her, leaving her pregnant and without either the fiancé or the other guy, who must've been a one-night stand or something equally unreliable.

Sex and passion. Even Abra Freakin' Holloway was vulnerable when it came to basic human nature.

As for him and her and what they'd just been up to... He didn't like being lumped in with every guy in the world, especially however many Abra had slept with. In fact, he didn't like thinking at all about however many Abra had slept with, or what she'd done with them, and he didn't want to know anything about who or what Abra had wasted her irresistible passion on.

Nope. Not one little detail. But he had to admit, she had a point about the two of them and just how much trouble they could get into if they let themselves.

"So," she added delicately, "if that means you rescind your offer and walk away, I understand. I would still hope you wouldn't, you know, call CNN first thing, but..."

He let a long pause hang between them. He knew what he had to say.

"Sweetheart, CNN was never on the table. I just wouldn't do that. But you are a beautiful woman, and I would be lying if I said I didn't find you awfully tempting. I'm sure you're used to that." He shoved his hands in his pockets as a reminder to keep them away from her. "After all, everybody likes you. It's part of the carefully constructed media package."

She bit her lip. "I said I was sorry."

"You're also right. You're pregnant, you're in a jam, and you couldn't be more off-limits," he offered in his most casual tone. "I'm a big boy. I can take the heat."

"You sure you're okay with that?" She ran both hands through her hair, holding it away from her face. "Because I can't promise I won't go crazy again and, well, do something stupid. I can't promise to be smart or sensible or rational. I have these hormones... I can't promise."

"I can. I'm one of the True Blue Calhouns," he said lightly. "My word is my bond."

"And when you say staying, you don't mean actually staying, as in here, in the same house, right? Because I know that wouldn't work."

"Overnight? I could protect you better..." But he knew she was right on that score. "No, I have a hotel room at the Illini Union. I'll keep it."

"Good." Exhaling with relief, Abra retreated even farther, and he noticed she was keeping her gaze well away from the table as she backed out of the kitchen. Aw, Abra. So easy to read.

"Not just good, this will be great," she declared. "Great. Hands off. No hanky panky. Just friends. Excellent friends. Who help each other in times of need. With things like cars and money and places to stay. Why not? I'll unpack and then you can tell me where we start from here."

He nodded, ready for her to leave the room and take her luscious curves with her so he could collect himself. But just when he thought he was clear, she popped back in.

"Sean?"

He looked up. "Yeah?"

"What exactly is a True Blue Calhoun?"

"I'll, uh, tell you later."

"Promise?"

"Yeah."

And then she really was gone. He could hear her dragging her Louis Whoever bags back to the bedroom to unpack. He should offer to carry the suitcases for her, but he needed to be out of her presence for a few moments to clear his head.

What the hell had he just signed up for?

7

"SHOULD WE MAKE A LIST?" Abra asked hopefully, pulling out her yellow pad and her favorite pen. "Steps we need to take to successfully slide me right into this undercover thing?"

Chewing on the end of the pen, she tried to wrap her brain around this as a fun makeover project with her as the subject, just to get herself motivated. Lists were always good motivators.

Besides, she was in a better mood than she had been in days. For one thing, Sean had done a run to the grocery store this morning and come back with plenty of Chunky Monkey. What a guy. For another, it was a lot more fun having someone else in on this mission with her, someone else to bear the burden of all those pesky decisions that had been stressing her out. She hadn't been out of the house yet since they'd struck up this partnership, and the idea that she could rest and hang out in perfect privacy while he went and secured the Chunky Monkey was lovely.

At the moment, Sean was distracted looking through her clothes for anything he considered suitable undercover attire, and he didn't even glance her way. She hoped that pair of scissors in his right hand wasn't going anywhere near the Gucci pants in his left.

"Sean, put down those scissors, somewhere safe," she commanded. "I don't care how disguised I'm supposed to be. You can't cut up a pair of $700 Gucci pants."

"Your clothes are unbelievable. None of this stuff is going to blend in on the streets of central Illinois in the middle of summer. Not to mention the fact that it all seems to be lined and long-sleeved and incredibly hot." At least he set aside the scissors, which meant she didn't have to hurtle herself between him and the pants.

"Lined, long-sleeved, and beautifully made," she amended. "Those pants also have a matching jacket and a corset dress. Gorgeous. I wore the dress and the jacket to the White House, for goodness' sake. And they were worth every penny." She waved the legal pad at him. "Sean? What about a list?"

"Uh, no," he said offhand. "Lists can be evidence later. General rule is to keep it in your head, not on paper and not on the phone. You don't have a computer or a PDA, do you? If you do, don't use it. Leaves a heck of a paper trail."

"Evidence? Like for what?" She couldn't keep the edge of alarm out of her voice. Using the word "evidence" sounded so grim, so criminal, so Martha Stewart.

But Sean quickly interrupted her thoughts. "Don't worry. Nothing like that."

How exactly did he know what she was thinking?

He went on, "Just if somebody spots you and starts to wonder if you are or if you aren't, and they go rooting around in your garbage and find samples of your handwriting, or a list that details your whole plan... Well, game over." His gaze narrowed. "You're sure it's just the tabloids, right? The cops aren't looking for you? No massive manhunt or anything?"

"From the police? Not as far as I know. I talked to Shelby before I left, so she knows I'm okay. Plus Julian did a press conference and said he wasn't worried. I think the only people looking should be the media. I already saw myself on the front of three different magazines at the supermarket." She chewed on a nail, recklessly ruining her French manicure. "Does it make a difference?"

"Well, it's not exactly normal," he explained, "but people have been prosecuted for trying not to be found if the authorities expend a whole lot of public funds searching. I just wanted to make sure nobody was doing that for you. As much fun as this is, I don't want to be aiding and abetting. Maybe I should at least check in and make some discreet inquiries, make sure there's no APB out on you."

"No," she said flatly. "You are not talking to anyone about any APBs. If you ask, they'll know you saw me."

"Abra," he began, but she stared him down, unwilling to budge on this one.

"No authorities."

"Okay. Maybe." Sean carelessly tossed aside her cigarette slim, beautiful aloe-green Gucci pants, the symbol of a different time. She probably couldn't get into them anymore, and wouldn't be able to for, oh, nine months... "You seriously don't own a pair of shorts? A T-shirt?"

"No," she returned hastily, collecting the pants and holding them close. "I bought the baseball hat and scarf at the airport, you know, for cover, but nothing else. I was trying to conserve my cash. I mean, my clothes were always under the coat, so no one could see them, and I really didn't think it was necessary to dress down as long as they were hidden." After that impromptu song-and-dance, even she wasn't convinced. She sighed. "Okay, I admit it. I'm lying. I didn't want to replace the clothes. I love the clothes."

"I know. You're a terrible liar," he muttered, still sifting through shirts and tops in a way she didn't appreciate. "I just don't get why you're hanging on to all this stuff when you can't wear it around here, anyway. Like the green suit. Where would you think you could wear that?"

"Will you please stop pawing my things?" She grabbed the adorable fitted jacket that matched the Gucci pants away from him and lovingly got the outfit back on the hangers before he could say anything. She remembered wearing that suit on *The Shelby Show*, the week when the topic was packrats who needed to clean house.

Cleaning house. Ridding yourself of unwanted baggage. It was so annoying when irony leapt up and bit her on her Gucci pants.

"The truth is," she admitted, "I'm having a hard time parting with some of this stuff. It's a link to my life at the top, brief as it was, and I guess I'm just not ready to give it up yet."

"You better get ready," he warned. "If you want to

act anonymous, the pointy high heels and the $700 pants aren't going to cut it."

"I know." She took a deep breath. "I should've left it behind. But the hair and the makeup were hard enough, and the jewelry... I mean, I gave Julian back his ring. Actually, I threw it at him, so *gave* isn't technically correct." She was gratified to see a smile curving Sean's lips. "Well, anyway, I walked away from all that. But I guess I'm having a little trouble with the rest. Like the shoes. I can't even wear them anymore—my feet have inexplicably gone up a size—and I have ten pairs of Manolo Blahniks and maybe five or six Jimmy Choos with me. If I showed you the boots..."

"eBay," he offered.

"eBay?" The idea made her feel stricken. "I can't sell my beautiful shoes on eBay!"

"You need the money and the shoes don't fit. eBay is practically anonymous. Seems like a no-brainer to me." He indicated a thumb at her suitcase. "I'd throw in the luggage, too."

"Oh, no! Not the Louis Vuittons." She shuddered. "I know you're right and they're a dead giveaway, and I should get over it and buy myself a piece of American Tourister at the discount store like everyone else. But I cannot part with my LV bags."

Sean wrinkled his brow. "I'm used to women being into shoes, but you're that emotionally attached to luggage?"

"It's just that Shelby gave it to me, like a welcome gift when I started making regular appearances on her show." Perching next to Sean on the bed, Abra fingered the smooth camel-colored leather trim on the largest suitcase. "I was so happy when I got it. I really felt like I had arrived at that exact moment, like whatever else happened in my life, no one could take away the fact that I had made it. It would be like admitting I was never going back to my real life if I gave it up."

"The sad thing is, I actually sort of understand that," he said ruefully. But he slid shut the valise, setting it carefully on the floor and out of sight. Then he turned to take her hand and draw her to her feet. "Let's stop moping over suitcases, okay? I say we get out of here."

The touch of his hands was enough to make her get tingly all over. Or maybe it was the proximity to a bed. Rumpled bedclothes, the smell of fine leather from her suitcase, Sean's warm, clever fingers on her wrist, sending shockwaves all the way up her arm...

Once again, her body leapt to red alert. Her mouth went dry, her head was whirling, and she couldn't quite catch her breath.

Luggage? Who cared about luggage? All she could think about was *him*.

Sheesh. If she didn't stop hungering for Sean at the drop of a hat, she was going to lose her mind. As she stared down at his hand wrapped around her wrist, her mind replayed that incredible, mind-blowing kiss in the kitchen. Although they had each cautiously toed the no-contact line since then, the kiss still zipped through her brain in slo-mo, in fast-mo, in real time, again and again. It would be so easy to tug him closer, to start it up again. She wanted more of it. Talk about sizzling her down to her toes. She honestly didn't know who had pushed it so far out of hand, but she had a feeling it was her. Hadn't she speculated that he would be an amazing kisser, with those perfect lips? And he was.

Plus there were the abs. Abra tried to remember to breathe in and out like a normal person. Her one chance to get a look at the abs and she'd blown it. Touching them had only made it worse because now they were branded in her imagination without actually having seen them or run her tongue over them...

Gulping, she quickly pulled her hand away from him, flexing her fingers, still wanting to dip under his shirt again and go where it lead. No matter how hard she tried to block the whole thing, she was drowning in *wanting*.

"Stay away from the six-pack," she hissed at herself. *You're pregnant. This is not the time for licking someone new. He's not yours. Stay away.*

"What did you say?"

"Um, I said, let's get out of here. I need some fresh air."

"Okay," he returned slowly. But they both knew that wasn't what she'd said.

At least they were getting out of the house now. That ought to be less risky, out in public where it wasn't so intimate, where she wasn't brushing into him every time she turned. Kitchen—off-limits because of the hot table fantasy and the smoking kiss and the three-second grope of a set of muscled abs that had felt like heaven under her hand. Bedroom—off-limits because he had touched her and swept her up and down with his intoxicating gaze, making her want to tumble right into the sheets. Pretty soon there would be nowhere in the house she could stay without disturbing mental images of Sean.

"Wh-where are we going?" she managed to ask.

"Out," he said tersely, carefully pulling his eyes up to meet hers. "Shopping."

She put on a heavily cheerful and nonchalant facade. "Oh, good. I love shopping. What are we buying?"

"Camouflage."

"You don't mean actual camouflage, do you? Like, the dark green and the beige swirls?" she tried. Not exactly her style.

"No, I don't mean actual camouflage." He lounged in the doorway, waiting for her, clearly uncomfortable being wedged into the small bedroom with her any longer. When he spoke, his words came quickly. "We want you to look like everybody else on a college campus in the middle of the summer. That's the absolute first step. I was thinking maybe the college bookstore. They sell all kinds of stuff. T-shirts. Shorts. Sweatpants. Hoodies. Enough to get by for now, anyway."

It was her turn to just say "okay" in a doubtful tone. He seemed awfully chatty all of a sudden. That was a lot of words strung together for quiet, intense Sean.

Next he pulled a pair of plain tortoiseshell glasses out of his pocket, acting studiously matter-of-fact and officious. "Oh, and I picked these up at the grocery store. They're actually reading glasses, but I took the weakest magnification, so you should be all right. A little disguise, but not hugely obvious as a disguise. As for the rest... You can leave on what you're wearing for now, but put the baseball cap on, too.''

Slipping on the glasses and her Orioles cap, testing the view, Abra smiled. She couldn't help it. The silliness of her situation had just struck home, what with the glasses blurring the edges of things a bit, Sean and that uncharacteristic torrent of words, and her initial concept of the two of them going shopping for camouflage. She could just see herself in army boots and fatigues.

Ah, well. It was shopping after all. And she got to go outside on a beautiful summer day. She counted the rest of her blessings. She hadn't been queasy for hours, even with a whole lot of leftover pizza and another pint of Chunky Monkey in her system. And Sean, her personal undercover expert, was turning out to be just what the doctor ordered. Except for the sex thing.

We are not thinking about sex, Abra. Hard abdomen, clever hands, delicious lips, slippery tongue... She sat back down with a thump. *We are not thinking about any of that.*

It was difficult to push her mind onto anything else when Sean was around, but she was going to have to try. Because he was right—the bottom line was that she needed him. It wasn't just that he was incredibly sweet and he knew what to do, but that he did grocery shopping, he provided nice little details for her disguise, and he didn't even make fun of her for being hung up on her hideously expensive French lug-

gage and her hideously impractical aloe-green
Gucci suit.

His words were occasionally gruff, but she could
tell he was enjoying their connection, too. He couldn't
really stop the half smile playing around his gorgeous lips, or the light in his eyes when he looked at
her. It was frightening. Sexy, but frightening.

Even more frightening was how much she trusted
him, even though she barely knew him. True Blue
Calhoun. Sean kept his own counsel most of the time,
he was smart as a whip, and yet he had that streak of
assurance—maybe even arrogance—that was so easy
for her to rely on.

Yep. With Sean in it, this was the best day she'd
spent since she'd found out she was pregnant. It
looked like getting found out by Sean Calhoun might
just have been a very lucky break.

SEAN SENT A GRIN Abra's way. She had her fancy
clothes and shoes stuffed in a plastic shopping bag as
she sniffed in the direction of Zorba's, a small restaurant promising gyros. She couldn't be hungry again,
could she? She certainly did pack it in for someone
her size. With her new University of Illinois T-shirt
tossed over some shorts and a pair of flip-flops, she
looked about eighteen, and like she actually belonged
on campus.

"You're practically beaming, Sean. You are so
proud of yourself," she teased. "Sean Calhoun,
makeover expert."

"Hey, you look wonderful. And about a million

times less miserable than when I saw you the first time, suffocating in that heavy coat."

"If only the school colors were something other than orange and blue," she lamented, looking down at her T-shirt. "No one looks good in orange."

"Stop it. You look great."

"Good enough, anyway." Head held high, she stepped smartly away from the window, doing a squeaky twirl in her flip-flops as if to model her new outfit. "Just in from Paris, les flip-flops et les gym shorts."

"All right. Let's not go nuts here." Sean casually glanced up and down the street, just to check for anyone suspicious. "No reason to call attention to us."

"You already know there's no one else on the street," she whispered, leaning closer. "C'mon, Sean, I've spent the last five years trying my hardest to catch people's attention. Give me a few minutes, okay?"

He attempted to hold back his smile. "I didn't know you had to try. I thought your warmth, energy and sparkle jumped off the screen and into people's living rooms."

"Oh, no. You weren't supposed to read my press clippings," she said with a laugh. Moving closer, she impulsively linked her arm through Sean's to pull him away from Zorba's and down to the corner.

It was an innocent gesture, and he knew she was doing it just to keep their conversation private, but as she tipped her head closer to his, he couldn't help but feel a certain level of intimacy. And that same old electrical pull.

"But let me tell you," she added in a light tone, "it takes a lot of hard work to be that warm and energetic and sparkly."

"Right."

For Abra, those things came as naturally as breathing. He understood perfectly why fans responded to her on TV—she was easy to look at, that was for sure, but she was funny and smart, too, incredibly empathetic, and she had this amazing spark that seemed to come from her very soul. Somehow she managed to be make him feel as if she were completely interested, as if had her undivided attention whenever she turned those golden hazel eyes his way. Warm and energetic? Absolutely. Jumping into your living room as your new best friend? Yep. Made perfect sense to him.

But as they crossed the street and moved toward the Quad again from a different corner, her mood seemed to change. A chill opened up between them even as her grip on his arm tightened.

What was up with that? As they cruised by the Alma Mater statue, a campus landmark, she hesitated, giving it a good once-over, frowning slightly at the tall bronze women, arms outstretched, with what appeared to be a large chair yawning behind her.

"The legend I always heard was that if a virgin walked by, the lady in the front would sit down in that chair," Abra noted coolly. "Did they tell you that, too? I guess in my current condition, she's not in any danger of sitting down for me."

Even as a joke, it was a pretty limp excuse for humor. "They told everyone that. And you know what? The lady never sat down for anyone."

"I know. It's just... I keep getting hit with memories. It was a weird time back then." Picking up her pace, she steered them into a U-turn and headed resolutely back to Campustown. She frowned. "I came back here for that reason, to kind of connect with the past, figure out where and why things went wrong. It's just harder than I thought. I'm not sure I know who that person was at all. The one who enrolled here in the first place, I mean. The one who wanted so desperately to *be* somebody."

"Oh, yeah?" He knew if he asked her directly why that was, she would clam up. But if he let her just keep talking, there was no end to what he could learn. So he bided his time.

Abra cocked her head to one side, turning back to send him a quick glance. "Do you think we were here at the same time? That would be strange, wouldn't it?"

"Not really." Dropping her arm, Sean moved directly behind her to wait for the light to change so they could cross the street, setting his hands casually on her shoulders.

He hadn't meant anything by the gesture, just a little protection from the street and any cars that might come by. But that palpable physical connection between them, the one he had come to expect, arose immediately. As if she didn't even realize she was doing it, she shifted closer, her back barely grazing his chest, her hair under his chin, and he had to grind his teeth and stare straight ahead to focus.

He'd forgotten what it was she was saying, but he let the words tumble out on automatic pilot. Something about being a student here... "There are what, thirty-five thousand students here? I would say I never met at least thirty-four of my fellow students. So if we were here at the same time, it's likely we never ran into each other."

"And where did you spend most of your time?" she asked softly. "I doubt you were the same places I was."

"I don't know." He considered that for a second, unable to come up with an interesting answer. Did it matter? Their conversation—their individual pasts— were so unimportant compared to the way she smelled, the way she felt, the way she was standing there with him *now*. They might be barely touching, but she was making a major impact on him from top to bottom.

"So, where were you as a student, Sean?" she asked again. "Frat? Dorm? Apartment? What was your major?"

Aware he wasn't keeping up his end of the conversation, he mumbled, "No frat for me. Yes to the dorm and then a house with five other guys. It was a zoo. My major? It changed a lot, but I guess mostly I stayed in liberal arts. History, poli sci, that kind of thing. One stint in the College of Commerce. But most of my classes were on the Quad. How about you?"

"Oh, I was a psych major as long as I was here. Which wasn't long." The light changed, and she stepped into the street, breaking the contact between them. She seemed distracted when she said, "So, you know, Psychology Building. But other than that, yeah, I was on the Quad a lot, too." She fixed him with a self-deprecating smile. "I guess that's why I was drawn back to it, for my contemplation, meditation, and morning sickness phase. Which was when you saw me." Stopping when she hit the curb, she turned back to him, focusing her gaze on him more intently. "Why did you change your major so much? What do you major in to be a cop, anyway?"

"I didn't want to be a cop then."

"No? I thought it was the family business."

"Which is exactly why I didn't want to do it," he told her. He set his jaw. "My dad was already a commander then, and Jake was headed straight for the force, which made me want to do anything else. I flirted with prelaw, premed, computer science, business. And ended up a cop, anyway."

"Huh."

Sean wasn't really happy being under her microscope. He could already see the wheels turning, and he knew reams of advice would be coming soon. That was apparently how Abra got herself off topics she didn't want to deal with, like the chemistry problem that kept cropping up between the two of them, or her regrets about her murky past. Good strategy. Unfortunately, however, he didn't really want to be dissected.

So he pressed a finger to her lips to head her off at the pass. "Before you start, I don't need career counseling. I may've resisted, but I found out where I fit. I'm a detective. I'm good at it. I like it. It surprised me as much as anyone, but I'm sticking."

With a mischievous expression, Abra bit down gently on his finger. "I think you would be good at anything you set out to do, Sean." He could feel the flick of her tongue against the very tip of his finger every time she hit a "th." And then she licked him on purpose, from about halfway down his finger back to the top.

Suddenly, with her wet pink tongue sliding over his finger, the mood shifted again. In fact, it felt as if the cement sidewalk had shifted under his feet. He sucked in his breath. "You're playing with fire, Abra."

Her gaze was a smoky topaz as she breathed, "I know."

"Abra?"

"Uh-huh."

"I'm going to kiss you. But casual, okay? Friendly. It's not going any further than that," he murmured, letting his lips hover an inch from hers. "It's good cover. Just two regular people, nobody special, sharing a pretty summer afternoon, maybe a kiss. Or two."

"Sean, no one is watching." But she looped her arms loosely around his neck, closed her eyes behind those fake glasses, and tilted her head to line up for the kiss. "We don't need cover."

"You always need cover," he whispered. He bent in that extra inch, barely brushing her moist, delicious mouth, just enough to taste her. Nothing wrong with that, was there?

"Sean..." She swallowed. She cleared her throat,

but her voice still came out husky and raw. "You don't know... You don't know what you do to me."

But it was obvious. "Your glasses steamed over."

She swore under her breath. He could see her nostrils flare and her breasts rise and fall as she breathed deeply, trying to get some oxygen to her brain. Ripping off the glasses, she lifted her hands to press hard against her temples, in what was a pretty adorable gesture of frustration. He was sure she didn't realize that it only pushed her breasts higher, fuller, making the luscious mounds that much more provocative. He looked away and jammed his hands into his pockets to keep himself from reaching for her.

"I guess there's no such thing as a casual kiss between us, huh?" he asked mournfully.

"Guess not." She rammed the glasses in her pocket. Her voice dropped even lower when she added, "I'm like a puddle here. One more minute and I may just end up begging you to make love to me, right here on the street."

And there was no way he would've said no if she had. Public indecency be damned. But out loud, he told her, "We can't have that."

She bit down hard on her bottom lip. "Nope. You promised, Sean. Remember?"

With a small sigh, Sean turned away. He took her hand, he lifted it to his lips, just to show her he understood, and then he started to amble down the sidewalk, pulling her with him, their hands still clasped. The two of them, walking along together... He was shocked to realize how natural, how right it felt.

Maybe it had started out as cover, for them to look

like any other couple, but it was beginning to feel like something more. Something very real.

She was Abra Holloway, golden girl, star. He was just a cop from Chicago trying to do a good deed. She had more baggage than the Louis Vuitton factory, and he was a solitary man who had enough trouble with the pesky entanglements of the family he was born with to even consider starting one of his own. Not exactly a match made in heaven.

So why did it feel like one?

8

"YEAH, OKAY. IF HE checks in, tell him to call me, okay?" Sean put his hand over the phone, sliding his gaze around to get a bead on Abra's whereabouts. Since she'd expressly told him not to do this, he thought it was better if she didn't overhear.

Come on. He was a big boy. He got to decide whether he wanted to risk aiding and abetting a fugitive, didn't he? What could it hurt just to verify that she wasn't on America's Most Wanted at the post office?

So he'd sneaked out to the screen porch to put in a quick call to his brother Jake, who was unfortunately still not back at the office or at home or answering his cell phone. Even Cooper, second choice at best, was also unavailable. Probably at the fishing cabin, out of signal range.

Damn it. How was a guy supposed to run a discreet check on the official response to Abra's absence if he couldn't get through to anyone he could count on not to ask questions?

Maybe Bill would be okay. He was a pal, another detective who'd come up about the same time. It wasn't like family, but Sean figured he could trust him. And at least he was in the office.

"Hey, Bill. It's Sean," he said, keeping his voice casual and unconcerned. "Listen, I'm out of town and I wondered if you could check on something for me. Just between us, okay?"

Bill's voice came booming over the wire. "I thought you were gone fishin' with the bros. What happened? Somebody stealing your trout and you need some backup to take 'em down?"

"Funny. No. The fishing trip didn't happen. Something else came up. Something personal."

"That sounds interesting. I didn't know you had a personal life, Sean." He chuckled. "So what do you need? Background check to see if your hot new girlfriend has a solicitation record?"

"Nah. No hot new girlfriend," he said quickly. "Sorry to disappoint you. Nothing important, really. Just..." Adding a sheepish tone to his voice, he improvised, "My mom is a big fan of that TV star, Abra Holloway, and she was dying to know if there was anything new on her vanishing act. You know my ma."

"Yeah. We all know your ma," Bill noted gruffly. "She tried to fix me up with one of your cousins at the mayor's picnic last summer. Jeez. You have my sympathies, pal."

"So you understand my problem." Sean found a laugh of his own. "She wants something, she doesn't give up. Anyway, she wanted me to find out about this Holloway disappearance, and I told her I would. So, anything come in on Abra Holloway? APB, maybe? Any kind of search going?"

"Abra Holloway," Bill mumbled. "Okay, I wrote

myself a note. Haven't seen anything. Let me check and get back to you."

"Good enough." He paused. He shouldn't be doing this, but he had this gut instinct… "Oh, and Bill? Anything else you can find on her, let me know, okay? Anything at all. But keep it on the down-low."

"Sure thing."

Behind him, he could hear the jingle of keys, and he quickly closed the phone, ignoring the beep that said he had messages. He knew they would all be from his mother, anyway, demanding to know how the search for the woman from the park bench was going. He felt a momentary twinge of guilt to be using his mom as a cover story while he wouldn't even take her calls, but it was only momentary. He told himself he would dutifully check her messages later. For right now…

"What are you up to?" he asked Abra, who was dressed in pale orange tie-dyed sweat pants and a matching tank top with U of I stretched tight across her breasts. She seemed to be getting into her new fashion statement. Looking at the way the shirt hugged her curves, so was he. He could totally get into—and under—that shirt, given half a chance.

"I thought I might go out." She shook his key ring. "Mind if I take your car?"

"Where to?"

"Nowhere," she said vaguely. "Maybe the grocery store."

"Out of Chunky Monkey again?" he asked with a smile. "Don't you think I should come with you?"

But she frowned. "I don't need a baby-sitter every minute, Sean," she shot back, surprising him with her

ferocity. He'd thought they were getting along so
well, and he was ready to give himself a gold star for
doing such a good job of keeping his hands to himself. More than a gold star. He deserved a freaking
Good Conduct medal.

"I'm not your baby-sitter," he argued. "I'm saving
your frisky little behind." But she waved him off.

"I'm learning the lessons, aren't I? Sooner or later,
I'm going to be doing this on my own, without you.
Might as well make a trial run," she grumbled.

Hmm... She was feeling feisty and independent all
of a sudden. *On my own, without you.* They both knew
that would happen eventually. Why did it bother
him? And why had she chosen now to get up on her
high horse? He narrowed his gaze, but he did his best
not to sound too concerned. "Sure. Whatever. Don't
be gone too long. And get milk, okay? You need the
calcium."

"Will you stop reading that damn book?" She spun
around, glaring at him. "I can read my own pregnancy book, thank you very much."

"I didn't read the book. It's just common sense."
He couldn't resist calling out, "Wear the glasses and
the hat!" as she stomped back into the house, her flip-
flops slapping in an angry rhythm. "And don't be
gone too long. I don't want to have to come looking
for you."

Without glasses or a hat, she poked her head back
onto the porch. "You're driving me nuts, Sean."

A few seconds later, he heard the echo of the front
door slam.

"Yeah, well, the feeling is mutual," he said grimly.

Looked like the frustration level was rising around here.

And sooner or later, something had to give.

"I STILL DON'T THINK pizza is good for you." Sean leaned across the wooden table in the mostly empty restaurant, giving her one of his most ominous faces.

Abra just smiled back at him and chewed on a breadstick with carefree abandon. "We're here. We've ordered. We can't take it back now."

She was getting pretty good at getting around him and his objections to her eating habits, even if he was still quite infuriating about it. She kept having to bite her tongue before she demanded just whose pregnancy this was, anyway. Aggravating, pushy, ridiculous man.

A traitorous little voice piped up to remind her that he was also beautifully put-together with abs to die for. "Who cares?" she asked under her breath, gnawing on the breadstick to beat the band.

She didn't care. Not her. She preferred to concentrate on the pushy, arrogant part of the equation rather than think about the abs or any of the other good parts. It was easier to avoid drooling on him that way.

After polishing off that hunk of bread, she reached for more. If the Princess Horny phase of her pregnancy didn't end soon, she was going to weigh 600 pounds, what with grabbing for food every time she thought about sex. Since she thought about sex every time Sean so much as breathed in her hemisphere, she was eating a ton.

It didn't help that she'd deliberately bought every last piece of bad stuff she wanted on her solo trip to the store. Chips, salsa, ice cream bars, frozen French fries... That and about ten magazines and newspapers, none of which she had shared with Sean. Hey, a girl had a right to see what the papers were saying about her, didn't she?

"None of it good," she murmured. There was lots of speculation about where she was, with theories ranging from a drug habit and rehab somewhere to a pilgrimage to Tibet, an illicit love affair with Ben Affleck, Eminem or Prince William, taking up religious orders, or fighting some dread disease in a clinic in Venezuela. The truth was starting to sound pretty tame by comparison.

There were also quotes all over the place from Julian. *I hope she's back very soon, rested and renewed,* he kept saying. Rested and renewed. Like she didn't know what that meant. *I hope she comes to her senses and stops this pregnancy nonsense and comes back so we can start being the perfect perennially-engaged-yet-unencumbered couple again.* "Not good at all."

"What's not good?"

"Nothing," she said brightly, pasting on a fake smile. She didn't want him to know about the collection of tabloids. Somehow she figured they would be against one of Sean's endless rules.

"You're not talking about the breadstick, are you?" he asked in confusion. "It's not good?"

"It's fine. It's delish." She dipped it in cheese sauce and took another healthy bite.

"I'm still not sure about the pizza. Too much salt, spicy, high in fat."

"Lay off the pizza," she growled. Now that she had acquired the complete camouflage kit, from shorts to sweats to a variety of University of Illinois T-shirts, even a sundress or two, she'd actually pushed him into taking her out to the pizza place instead of just ordering in, which was an improvement. In a celebratory mood, she'd even worn one of her new sundresses, which left plenty of room for her tummy. She was trying to maintain a positive attitude. It wasn't easy.

"Calm down, will you?" he put in.

"FYI, I did read the book on the issue of so-called junk food," she told him, ignoring the "calm down" thing, which he already knew she hated. "It says I can have it in moderation. I didn't have pizza yesterday. Therefore today is moderation."

"Abra," he began in a warning tone.

"Shh," she cut in with a warning of her own. "Don't say my name out loud. How many..." She dropped her voice to a whisper. "How many *Abras* are there out there, anyway? If anyone heard you, it would be, as you put it, *game over*."

"I don't know," he stage-whispered back. "How many are there?"

"Only three that I know of. Me, my grandmother, and the girl in *East of Eden*." Still feeling a tad put out, she inquired acerbically, "So, Sean, how did you get to be such a pregnancy expert, anyway? Do you have a wife and four kiddies at home you haven't told me about?"

"Uh, no. But I rode around in a squad car for eight months with an expectant father as my partner," he countered. "Plus in my experience, cops tend to be a procreating bunch, so I've had lots of friends in that position, as well as cousins and even a couple of aunts. Oh, yeah." He lifted a jaded eyebrow. "And my mother is nuts about babies. She can't keep her mouth shut on the subject. Believe me, I've heard more about the intimate side of pregnancy and childbirth than I ever wanted to know."

"The intimate side? How intimate?"

Although she'd read the part of the book about sex so many times the pages were dog-eared, she had so far avoided all the unpleasant warnings about the things her body was going to be going through month by month. But she was really going to have to plan ahead and map out her future sooner or later. It was so easy to fall into the endless game of sparring with Sean, mooning over Sean, thinking about Sean... And block all the icky details out. As if nausea and dizziness, suddenly contending with C cups (perilously close to D's) when she'd been a B all her life, swollen feet, and obsessing about sex weren't bad enough.

"You probably shouldn't tell me what's coming," she decided. There were things she really didn't want to talk over with Sean. "I'm not going to want to know, am I?"

"Sure you are." His smile was encouraging, but it just made her notice the cute way his lips peaked in the middle and that wasn't going to get her anywhere.

What did she have to do? Get a blindfold? But she would still be able to smell him. And feel him. She groaned.

"Hey, stop worrying," he told her. "There's good stuff coming up."

She spared a gloomy glance his way. "So you have lots of police friends with babies?"

"Yeah. Lots."

After dropping an uneaten lump of bread onto her plate, she propped her elbows on the table and leaned over a little. "I wondered about that. Because they're in these dangerous jobs, putting their lives on the line, right? Yet they somehow manage to move forward, bringing babies into this world. And they even make it work somehow, day in and day out." She shook her head. "I'm in awe."

Sean's eyes were so blue, so alight with sympathy. "You'll be a great mother."

"Me? I haven't really had time to think about that part yet." She stared down into her water glass. "So far, I've been worried about how to be pregnant, not how to be a, uh, mother." Even the word freaked her out. "A mother. Good grief. Me?"

"You're doing fine, sweetheart. You will do fine. C'mon." Sean ventured a hand across the table to clasp hers. "If someone were sitting in front of you in your position, asking for your advice, what would you tell her? You'd say she should read the books, see a doctor, follow the instructions, take a deep breath, relax, and go from there. Right? You're doing most of that. You're doing fine."

Keeping her voice low, Abra whispered back, "I

thought you'd never seen me on the show. How do you know what I would say?"

"I know you." He squeezed her hand. "Besides, that's the advice my mother has given every single one of my cousins and cousins-in-law who've had babies, and they are about twenty of them."

"Hmm..." She regarded him with curiosity. "So your mother doesn't have any grandchildren yet? Just grandnieces and nephews?"

Sean pulled away, shifting his weight to balance on the back legs of his chair. "Yeah. It's tough," he said with a touch of irony. "She's always trying to match me up with somebody's daughter or somebody's neighbor. She thinks if they can make meat loaf, I ought to marry them."

"Meat loaf being a high priority?"

"When it comes to potential wives for me, breathing is about all she needs to see," he returned dryly. "Anything else is gravy."

Abra laughed. "Your mother sounds great, Sean. I know she gets on your nerves, but I think everyone should have a mother like that, who really cares about them enough to meddle. At least a little."

Sean regarded her thoughtfully. "You don't?"

"Not really." She shrugged. "Don't get me wrong. My mother is a lovely person. It's just, I don't really keep in touch."

He didn't ask, just lifted an eyebrow in an unspoken question.

"You could say," she drawled, circling around an answer, "that I was headstrong and disappointed my parents early on and we haven't been incredibly close ever since."

"I find it hard to believe they're not busting their buttons over you and your show and all your success," he said slowly. "Who wouldn't be thrilled to see their daughter as the toast of TV?"

She wrinkled her nose. "They look at it as more of an embarrassment than anything else. 'Why, Betsy darling, did Cynthia Sheffield say that your younger daughter is on television? How droll.' 'Why, yes, I believe she is.' Followed by a polite cough and a firm change of subject." Speaking of which... "How about your brothers? Are they like you? The idea of three of you running around sort of boggles the imagination."

"Like me? In some ways. We all have the True Blue thing going." As he used that same, mocking tone, she knew *he* knew exactly what she had done to switch the focus of the conversation.

"I love the True Blue thing," she said honestly.

"We didn't really have a choice," he explained, "being my father's sons. My mom always complains that he can't help but try to solve every problem he runs across, whether it's his business or not. And she's not so different, even though she would never admit it. But if a baby or somebody's kid is involved, there is no way she wouldn't jump in."

She couldn't take her eyes off him. It wasn't even the sensual pull so much as the virtue and goodness fairly shining through him. "Gee, that sounds like someone else I know."

"I told you. The True Blue thing."

"So," she said briskly, still trying to get to the bottom of his family dynamic and stay away from her own, "does your mom try to match up your brothers all the time, too?"

"Not really," he allowed. "She thinks Jake is too much like my dad, too controlling, too set in his ways, not a good candidate for the women she likes, and Cooper is the opposite—too much of a flake. Irresponsible, crazy, you know. So she pretty much concentrates on me."

"Interesting," she mused, drawing out the word. "So you must be her favorite."

"I guess so." He started to rock a little on his chair. "My dad relies on Jake. My mom relies on me. And Coop..." He scowled. "We all know better than to rely on Cooper."

Given the nervous business he was doing with the chair, she could tell he was uncomfortable with all this scrutiny. So she smiled and purposely lightened the tone. "Well, I would love to meet your mother. And your brothers and your dad, too."

"Nah, you don't want to do that," he said quickly.

"I don't?" she asked. "But they all sound terrific. Oh." She nodded. "I get it. You don't think they would like me."

Sean's eyebrows rose. "I thought everybody liked you. Carefully constructed media package and all."

"Yeah, well, not your matchmaking mother who would certainly want someone better than a slutty pregnant woman with a checkered past hanging around her favorite son." Abra began to rip a breadstick into tiny pieces. "I can just see her welcoming me with open arms. More like welcoming me with a can of Mace and a restraining order."

"Man, are you off-target." Sean reached over and stilled her hands, stopping her from destroying any more of the bread. "I was thinking that before I could even introduce you, she would be picking out your wedding dress and calling up all her friends to tell them I was finally going to give her those grandchildren she's dying for. I can't imagine you sitting still for that. Seeing as how we're not in a, uh, relationship like that."

"Of course not. We're not in any kind of relationship," she agreed. "I mean, friends. But that's all. No one would ever think we were anything more than that, because—because it just isn't possible. Right?"

"Right."

"So we would hardly want your mother leaping to any other conclusions."

"Exactly."

She still thought his mom sounded like a lot of fun, but she understood his trepidation now. Sort of. Would it be so terrible for his mother to assume that they were...involved? And if she did think Abra was actually *with* Sean, in the sense of his girlfriend or something, would she really be as enthusiastic as he assumed? Or would she take one look at Abra and tell her never to darken her door again?

"Believe me, my mother would love you," he assured her. "My dad and Jake might run a few background checks, just to be sure, but I think they would come around pretty quickly. Whereas Cooper would be all over you. He thinks he's a real player. Coming up against someone like you..." Sean shook his head. "He'd be trying to take you home with him in five seconds."

"Yeah, sure." Like anybody would be coming on to her in her current condition.

"You really don't know, do you?"

"Hmm? Know what?" What was he talking about? "It doesn't matter. I still say you make them sound like a lot of fun," she contended. She tilted her head, considering him and his family. "Sean, I can understand not really liking the interference, but have you thought of discussing it with them and setting boundaries? Rather than just shutting them out, I mean?"

That confused him. He lowered his brow, staring at her. "Who said I shut them out?"

"Well, you did," she responded. "Think about it. They're all cops, so you don't want to be. Your mother wants you to go on what you think is a fool's errand and you do it, anyway, just to get away from her and her matchmaking. You have a choice of being on vacation with your brothers or fooling around with me, and you choose me. Hmm... Does he pick the family who know him like the back of their hand? Or does he pick hanging out with someone who is the very definition of unavailable, who is so wrapped up in her own problems she is not going to look too closely at him?"

"Wait a minute..."

"I've got you pegged," she told him. "It's not brain surgery, Sean. It's just listening."

"Listening, huh?" Once again, he leaned over the table, taking both her hands in his. He bent down to press a kiss in her palm, but for once, she wasn't so easily distracted.

"I think you depend on them a lot more than you are willing to admit," she concluded with some spirit. "I think if anyone threatened any one of the Calhouns, you would leap into the fray, no questions asked, sword drawn. It would be over so fast the other guy wouldn't stand a chance."

"Leap into the fray?" he echoed, clearing making fun to keep her from analyzing him any further. "What kind of fray would that be? With swords? What, we're working Medieval Times?"

She didn't have to answer, because the waitress arrived at that moment with a huge round silver platter, brimming over with pizza.

"Hey, lovebirds, break it up," the girl announced with a laugh, waving at them to untangle and get their arms off the table. "I need a place to put this."

"Yum, yum, yum," Abra murmured, closing her eyes and savoring the smell as the waitress slid the pan into the center of their small table.

"One thing about you. Food will get you off just about any track," Sean noted. "It's pretty handy how that works."

"Oh, pooh. Nothing wrong with appreciating your food." She already had a piece on the way to her mouth. "She who hesitates is lost."

Sean lifted his hands in the air, surrendering. "I like a girl with a healthy appetite. And you sure have one. Now if we could just it get directed at something better than ice cream and pizza."

"Like what?" she taunted. *Like you?* was the unspo-

ken follow-up. Thank goodness it remained unspoken. But she got punished for even thinking it. Pizza,
hot from the oven, met the soft tissue in her mouth
with an audible sizzle. "Yeow. My *mouth!*"

Scalding cheese had practically burnt a hole in her
upper palate. She dropped the slice like a hot potato,
using both hands to fan in front of her mouth. Perfectly calm, Sean handed over her glass, and she
sloshed cool water around the injury.

"Yeow," she said again, although not quite as loud
or shrill this time, poking at the injury with her
tongue. Not too bad.

"So maybe instead of 'she who hesitates,' you
should go with 'haste makes waste' next time?" he inquired. His lips quirked as he tried not to laugh at
her.

"Very funny." She gave him a very good imitation
of a glower. "You didn't warn me it was so hot, Sean.
You wanted me to burn my mouth to shut me up. It's
all your fault."

He blew carefully on his own piece. "Wait a minute. When did I turn into the princess's official taster?
Now you want me to be the early warning system for
burns? Poison, too? I think I should be insulted."

"You aren't insulted," she said in a pooh-poohing
tone, grinning at him.

"I'm not?"

All in all, this had been a great evening out so far.
They'd sort of had a fight about his continued med-
dling in her diet, she'd found out all kinds of new
things about him and his family, and they had en-
tered a new phase of lighthearted banter, about pizza

of all things. Once she let herself relax, it was actually...fun. Which was something she just wasn't that used to.

"I think you're harder to insult than that, Sean. But I'll keep trying."

Sean laughed out loud. She liked seeing him that way. But it was dangerous to think about how much. So she cut her pizza into tiny bites, concentrating on blowing on it as it hung on the end of her fork, before chomping into it again with gusto.

His slice dangled from his fingers. "You really do like this pizza, don't you? Even with a burnt mouth?"

"Love it."

Casually, mostly looking at his plate, he asked, "Did you like it when you were a student, too? Is this one of the things you're revisiting?"

"What?" She hadn't anticipated this conversational turn. "Oh, I didn't eat much pizza then," she answered without thinking. "When I was a freshman, I was, you know, eating dorm food and worrying about my weight, so it was all salads. Every meal, salads. Then I got married, so I was trying to be all Susie Homemaker, inventing new tuna-noodle casseroles and making my own bread. I've always been a terrible cook, but I didn't poison him, and my lack of cooking skills were not why he dumped me, so don't even think..." She broke off, only now realizing what she'd said.

But Sean was on it like a Doberman on a chew toy. "You were married? As in, vows, priest, *married* married?"

She bit down hard on her lower lip. The cat was out of the bag. And she had no idea what to say next.

9

SHE REACHED FOR HER CUP and took a big gulp of water as a stalling tactic.

"Come on," Sean ordered. "Spill it. You were really married?"

"Well, yeah." Why, oh, why, hadn't she thought before she spoke? There was no reason for Sean or anybody else to know about all that ancient history. The hole she was digging for herself just kept getting bigger and bigger. What could she say now to explain it? She had to say something. "I mean, yes, I was married. When I was a sophomore. For about five minutes. No biggie."

He looked stunned. "Wow."

Abra played with the edge of her pizza, poking at a sausage with her fork. "Okay, not five minutes. More like a few months." She hazarded a glance his way, desperate to recapture the fun, casual mood of a few minutes ago. She threw a hand in the air, trying to make it sound like any other item on her resume. "So now you know about my misspent years as a noncollege student. I did a whole three semesters before I dropped out to get married. Young, stupid... You know, it happens."

"And, uh..." Sean's eyes held her, steady, curious, oh so blue. "Who was he?"

It just kept getting worse, didn't it? "One of my psychology professors," she confessed.

"Your professor?"

It was only if she pretended it didn't mean anything to her, all carefree and blasé, that she could go on. "He was forty. I was nineteen. So, that pretty much says it all. I thought I was in love." She offered a quick, hollow laugh. "Maybe I was. Who knows? I was definitely bowled over. I mean, here I was, this silly little freshman psych student, all enthused to be a shrink some day and you know, *help* people. And he was a professor. He was smart and sophisticated—to me, anyway—I mean, he wrote the textbook for my first psych class! I was so flattered that he picked me out of that huge class."

But Sean was back a few pages. "Wait a minute," he said, with a murderous gleam in his eye. "Let me get this straight. He was forty? You were his *student?*"

"Sean, it was a long time ago," she tried. "I appreciate the righteous indignation on my behalf, but I was of legal age, you know. And we followed the rules and did not date until after I was out of his class. Really."

"That's a real plus."

"So now you know why I don't talk about it." She tapped her fork against her plate, making a pinging noise. "It's kind of ugly. And dumb. Honestly, ever since I've been Abra Cadabra, media darling, I've kind of expected someone like my freshman roommate or his ex-wife or even his current wife to come out of the woodwork. Abra's Past—The Tacky Teen Marriage She's Hiding! Read all about it!"

"And was this the headstrong bit that disappointed your parents?" he asked quietly.

She nodded. "I didn't tell them till after I was married. They said it was a huge mistake and I would be really sorry. And I was. So bonus points for them."

"But no reconciliation with Mom and Dad after it fell apart?"

Shaking her head, Abra frowned. "I wasn't in the mood for I-told-you-so's. Besides, my parents are big in the 'You made your bed, now lie in it' school of child-rearing. So I moved away and didn't really stay in contact. It was just easier."

"So what happened? To the marriage, I mean." Sean's voice was so low, she had to bend closer to even hear. Apparently even he thought this was an embarrassing story, not fit for other ears. Luckily they were in a mostly empty restaurant, with no one even within eyeshot at the moment. There were maybe a few people upstairs in the carryout section within earshot if she really shouted. So she figured they were safe as long as the waitress wasn't lurking.

"Oh, you want to know about the end of it? Not pretty." This time her laugh was bitter. "Surprise, surprise, the tale of Little Abra and the Professor gets worse. It also ties in rather nicely to my current situation."

"How so?"

Abra edged her chair around, pretending to scan the cavernous room for the absent waitress. "I'm not allowed to drink while I'm pregnant, am I? Because I could sure use a stiff one right about now."

"No, you're not allowed to drink." His voice became more soothing. "Come on. Just tell me."

Giving in, she pulled her chair back around. "You know most of it already. I dropped out in the middle of my sophomore year, we got married, and then the other shoe dropped." She pushed away her plate, but Sean leaned across the table, slipping his hand over to frame her face, rubbing his thumb softly against her cheekbone in a gesture that was oddly comforting, especially since she felt pretty untouchable right now. She could feel liquid pooling in her eyes, and she willed herself not to cry. Damn hormones.

"What other shoe?" he asked kindly.

"I went in to the health service for birth control, being a new bride and thinking it might be good to wait for a little while before I got pregnant." She cast her eyes down at her hands in her lap. "Imagine my surprise when the doctor told me I didn't need to worry about birth control. Ever. He was one hundred percent sure I would never conceive."

"But..."

"But my brand-new husband wanted a large family," she went on, starting to feel more wounded by the minute, bringing up all the old, bad news. She brushed Sean's hand off her cheek and a tear away at the same time, sitting up straighter in the hard, wooden chair. "He was really angry that I had deceived him into thinking I would be all, you know, fertile and fecund. I guess he expected me to be popping babies out like a Pez dispenser. In fact, he told me that was the reason he'd hooked up with me in the first place, because his ex-wife had said definitely no kids. They broke up over it, so he decided to start over with a younger, more compliant model. That was me, then. Funny how people change. Nobody would call me *compliant* now, would they?"

"Not if they were paying attention."

Abra twisted her lips into a smile. "Which he was definitely not. When we found out I couldn't have children, David annulled me before the ink was dry on the marriage certificate. I think he married one of his grad students within the year—someone more *compliant*, I guess—and they ended up with four or five kids. I kept track of him, just so I would never, ever end up anywhere near him. He moved her and the kids to a university in Toledo. Probably happy as a little family of clams."

"Okay, for starters, you were nineteen, so no way it was your fault. Second, you should be thanking God you dodged that bullet," he said flatly. "I heard all I needed to hear when you said he was twice your age and your professor. That's just wrong on so many levels."

She let her gaze linger on his clear, blue eyes, shining with anger, amazed that he was so totally on her side. Even with Shelby, her friend and mentor when it came to career issues, Abra had never really felt as if there were someone who always had her back, unconditionally, no questions asked. But that was the way it felt with Sean. She hadn't known him for long, but she knew without a doubt that he was with her, on her team, backing her up, no matter what. The thought made her heart swell, just a little, with tenderness.

"It was pretty awful at the time," she confided. "I felt like my life was over." She blew out a long breath. "Just think. If things had worked out the way I wanted then, right now I would be a faculty wife in Toledo with three kids and a nasty fifty-year-old husband who's probably still sleeping with his students."

"Yes, but…" He paused. "Abra, I don't mean to be king of the obvious here, but you *can* conceive."

"Yeah, I know. Big fat cosmic joke, isn't it? All these years, I've thought I couldn't." She set one hand at her waist. It was only a little thicker than before, but everything felt so different. "After a while, I kind of got used to the idea that motherhood wasn't going to happen for me, and I actually went looking for a man who didn't want children so he wouldn't be disappointed."

"And that would be Julian the Jerk?" Sean interjected sourly.

"That would be Julian. So imagine my surprise…"

"To find yourself expecting Julian's baby," he supplied.

"To find myself expecting Julian's baby." Abra managed a warmer smile for Sean, who now knew each and every one of her secrets. Phew. It felt good to get it off her chest, as if a huge burden had been released. Scary, but good. Maybe this was why she had returned to Champaign-Urbana, the place where her life had started to get offtrack. So she could shine a light on her old mistakes, expose them to the sun of a brand-new day, and move forward now with confidence and clarity.

"So what are you going to do?"

"The thing is, when I found out I was pregnant, I knew I wanted this baby. I know you think I'm avoiding doctors, but I did go, right at the beginning, both to confirm the pregnancy and also to make sure that I was healthy. I lied about my name, it was a free clinic, and I shouldn't have done it, but I wanted to be sure. This baby is a miracle for me, Sean. It was as if all those choices I didn't think I had came flooding back." She nodded, gaining confidence in her decisions by the minute. "So having the baby is a given. But my career... Where I go, what I do, how I manage to do it, that's all up in the air." Biting down on her lip, she peered at him across the table. "What do you think, Sean? What do you think I should do next?"

"You're asking for my advice?"

"Yeah, shocking, isn't it? Miss Know-It-All asks for advice," she said mockingly.

"I didn't mean it like that. It's just... I don't know what to tell you." He narrowed his gaze, considering for a long moment. "I have to say, running off and going underground seems kind of drastic. Surely your fans will still love you even if you admit you made a mistake. So you say, hey, the relationship with Julian the Jerk didn't work, but I'm thrilled to be a mother and I'm going forward from here. Hope you'll tune in to see me dispense advice to other new moms."

"Ah, yes, but Julian was supposed to produce my new show. Julian produces *The Shelby Show*. Julian is very much opposed to the idea of this baby," she countered. "What do I do about that?"

Sean lifted his wide shoulders in an elegant shrug under his black T-shirt. "The Jerk can be as opposed as he wants. Fact is, you're having the baby and there's nothing he can do about it."

"He can certainly not produce the show. He can certainly keep me off *The Shelby Show* forever and ever."

"Bad PR for him."

"Yes, but he says the baby isn't his. I know it's his; I'm positive, since he's the only person I've slept with." Her voice was rising as she got into the swing of her argument. It was so refreshing and energizing to be able to say out loud all the things that had been swimming in her head for the past three weeks. Wow. Only three weeks since she'd discovered she was pregnant. It felt like three years. "He knows he can make my life miserable. He already has! He told me he would spread it around that I slept with everyone up to and including the 6th Fleet, that given my supposedly trampy ways, there is no way to know who fathered this baby. What am I supposed to do, drag him on the *Maury* show for paternity tests?"

"Terrible PR for him if it comes to that," Sean argued.

"He doesn't care. He's not the one with an image to protect. I am." She pressed her lips together to keep herself from starting to curse like a sailor. Thinking about Julian and the terrible things he'd said really did bring out the worst in her. "If I push him, I lose, no matter what. But I don't care. I'm having this baby. I am."

"I believe you," Sean said quickly.

"You see, Julian hates being wrong. He also hates having his neat and tidy life disrupted." She exhaled. "I knew that. That's why we were good together. It was a neat and tidy engagement that was supposed to hang on forever."

"But you changed the rules."

"Yep." She lifted her chin with determination. "And I'm not changing them back." Forcing a laugh, she asked, "Isn't that a hoot? Hooked up with one guy who only wanted me if I could have kids, and one who only wanted me if I couldn't. Neither one cared about me, just my uterus."

"I can't believe that's true."

"But it is," she admitted. "So at the very least, I'm guilty of having terrible judgment about men. Which makes me look like an idiot, trying to tell other people what to do when I so clearly had no idea how to arrange a decent life for myself."

"Stop beating up on yourself. What are you, supposed to be psychic? I still say you go for it, you put the truth on the line and let the chips fall where they may." Looking very sure of himself, Sean smacked a fist into the table to make his point. "Your fans will follow you. And if they don't, too bad. You'll find something else to do."

"Yes, but—"

She didn't get to finish that thought. A loud clang, as metal hit the floor, interrupted them, and that was followed by shattering glass and hushed, urgent voices back by the cash register. Sean's gaze swept past her, zeroing in on the source of the noise, and he went very still.

"That sounded bad," she remarked, turning around in her seat. "Did someone drop a tray of glasses or something?"

"Don't look," Sean cut in. His voice was harsh and curt, brooking no objections. "Stay where you are, and look at me, okay? This way."

"Why are you acting so weird?" she asked slowly. "It's just a waitress dropping a tray, isn't it?"

His voice was soft, but very firm. "There's a guy by the cash register. All we can see from here is his back, but I think he's trying to rob the place. I think the waitress got spooked and dropped the tray."

"Come on, Sean. You can't know that." She twisted in her chair, but he pulled her back, dragging her hands front and center.

"Sorry!" the waitress called out in a strained, shrill voice, waving a hand at Sean. "Just dropped some stuff. Nothing to worry about."

"See?" Abra tried.

"Okay, listen." Clearly ignoring her, he focused on the scene unfolding behind her with deadly calm. "Right now, his back is turned and he can't see you. I'm going to go over there, nice and easy, and check it out. As soon as I stand up, I want you to pretend you dropped something and duck under the table, okay? Come around to my side and get under the table, behind the chairs."

"Sean, I—"

"Don't argue. Just do it." Noiselessly, he pushed

away from the table, moving at a deliberate, measured pace past her and toward the cash register at the other end of the long room.

Frozen to the spot, she almost didn't move. But Sean wouldn't have fallen into automatic cop mode if it weren't warranted, would he? He seemed so certain there was something wrong. As she tried to decide, she actually dropped her napkin completely by accident. Nerves or cosmic sign?

"Cosmic sign," she whispered, following the napkin down to the floor. Tucking herself into the small space under the heavy wooden table, she scooted around and peered through the slats of the chair so that she could see what was happening.

Her eyes widened and her heart dropped to her knees as Sean ever-so-casually approached the waitress and the strange man. Still apparently not clueing in on the fact that Sean was edging up behind him, the man kept waving his arms around as he ranted about something to the waitress. He was wearing a bandanna and a heavy flannel jacket that seemed inappropriate for the weather, and she suddenly realized what Sean had meant about how your clothes could make you look suspicious before you uttered a word. This guy totally looked suspicious. Heavy coat, bandanna. Which was just what she had worn that day on the Quad.

"At least I wasn't a robber," she groused.

Oh, lord. Was that a gun in his hand? Maybe just a cell phone. Abra pushed at the panic choking her, trying to remember to breathe. *Sean will take care of it, Sean will take of it,* she repeated to herself. *And please let that not be a gun, because Sean better not be throwing himself in the line of fire just to protect a few bucks at a pizza place.*

It's what he does, Abra, she reminded herself. *It's who he is.*

Yes, I know, she argued right back, *but does he have to do it right now?*

"Hi," he called out casually as he neared the pair by the cash register. "Could I get my check?"

The guy in the flannel shirt whirled around, the waitress shrieked, "Get out of here!" toward Sean, and that was all the time it took for Sean to jump the guy, smash him facedown into the cash register, and pin his arms behind him. Pans and pizzas went flying off the table, making a terrible clatter, and the waitress started to scream.

Abra felt like she was watching a movie. This couldn't be real. But what she now saw was absolutely, positively a gun scuttling across the floor, spinning harmlessly out of the way near the door to the restroom, as three more employees hurtled down the stairs from the carryout section of the restaurant and a pair of patrons from the other part of the restaurant wandered in to see what all the fuss was about.

Her heart was pounding so loudly she figured everyone in the place could hear it. No? Pressing her hand into her chest as a way to calm the frantic thumping, Abra tried to catch her breath. Sean had been magnificent. Magnificent. She'd never realized that a man in action could be a very powerful thing.

Right now, he had ripped the bandanna off the guy's head and he was tying his hands with it, giving him another clonk into the cash register for good measure when he started to mouth off, while the waitress sort of collapsed onto the floor and her friends from upstairs attended to her.

Holy smokes. Sean was so good at this. Totally in control, no wasted motion, all over in about five seconds.

She'd never seen anything like it. As if in slow motion, she crawled out from under the table, walked over to the place on the floor where the gun had skidded to a stop, and picked it up. It was small and silver, but heavier than she expected. She turned back to Sean. "Excuse me. I hate to bother you, but do you need this?" she asked, dangling it from two fingers, not really wanting to touch it.

"Abra, I told you to stay under the table," he said fiercely.

"Yes, but—"

"Okay, bring it over here, will you? You shouldn't be carrying it around. You could drop it. It could go off accidentally." Still hanging on to the robber with a lethal grip, Sean shoved the man onto the floor and put his knee in his back. With one hand still on the creep's neck, Sean reached up to take the gun from her, drawing the edge of his T-shirt away from his body to hold it, exposing those gorgeous abs of his and making her eyes widen even more.

Not a good thing to notice at this moment. A little dizzy, feeling as though her head were sort of floating, she backed away delicately.

"Abra, sweetheart, focus, okay?" His eyes held her,

steady and commanding. "I need someone to call 911. My cell phone is in my back pocket. Can you get it?"

Why was he acting like she was a wuss or something? Did she look like she was going to pass out just because of a little criminal activity and a small gun?

Oh, wait. She *was* going to pass out.

"Abra." Sean's tone cut through the fog in her brain. "Stay with me. Breathe. Please, sweetheart, I need you to stay with me, okay? I need you." Savagely, he barked, "Could one of you guys get this woman a chair, please? Before she faints? And somebody call the cops. But first get her a chair!"

"Hey, mister," one of the kids who worked there returned weakly, "I thought you were a cop."

"He is," Abra announced, pushing herself to concentrate. She was not going to faint. She refused. If she was in shock, well, that was just going to have to wait. Sean needed her to be strong, damn it. Retreating into crankiness to keep herself focused, she muttered, "Of course he's a cop. What was your first clue, Nancy Drew?"

There were more people milling around, including cooks and customers and passers-by, but no one was doing anything. Poor Sean had to hold the criminal down, secure the gun, and direct everyone else around all by himself.

She decided right then and there that she was not going to let Sean down, not after that performance. Didn't they realize that he had just saved all of their lives like it was another day at the office? Didn't they realize he was a hero? She grabbed the cell phone out of his back pocket and dialed 911.

"I'm at a pizza place on Green Street," she snapped into the phone as soon as someone answered. "There's been a robbery attempt. We were really lucky because a police officer from Chicago named Sean Calhoun took care of the whole thing. Can you get someone over here to clean it up, please? You need to take the, uh..." What was she supposed to call the creep on the floor? "You need to take the *bad person* away, and you need to give Sean a medal."

As the operator on the other end demanded her name, Abra hesitated, unsure what to do. She hadn't stopped to think about the implications of reporting a crime. She mumbled, "Just get someone over here, okay?" and snapped shut his phone.

"Are you all right?" Sean asked. He looked really worried, and she wanted to kiss him so badly it hurt. He went flying to take down criminals without a second thought and then he was worried about *her?* This man was incredible. He was a saint.

At that moment, she would cheerfully have kissed him, made love to him, married him, and had his babies, right there in the pizza joint.

"I'm fine now," she assured him. "Sean, do you want me to sit on him? So you can do, you know, whatever you need with the gun? Like, take the bullets out or something?"

Sean grinned at her. "Sit on him? No, I don't think so. We'll just wait till the locals arrive, okay?"

"Okay." She reached around behind him, awkwardly poking his cell phone into the back pocket of his jeans, trying to avoid touching his butt as she slid it back in there. He had a great butt, but the washboard abs were also on display, what with the twisted T-shirt, and she couldn't help gawking a little. Okay, a lot. That was the world's most beautiful six-pack, and her fingers ached to touch it. Just drinking in his flat stomach and hard, muscled abdomen, finally, after thinking about it so many times, she had to take a deep breath. But she couldn't look away.

"Abra?"

"Yes."

"That's fine, thank you," he said gently. "Why don't you sit down while we wait? I'm still a little concerned about you."

"No, I'm fine. Really." But she did it, anyway. Because she did need to sit down. Not as a result of lingering shock or aftereffects of the robbery attempt, but because every nerve ending in her body had suddenly jumped to life. They were all sending one overpowering message. *Take this man. Take him now.*

Sean's body, Sean's face, Sean's amazing superman stunt... Images whirled in her brain. She hungered for him. She was absolutely mad for him. She had thought she was turned on before, when they kissed, when he touched her, but it was nothing compared to this, this flood of longing, this desperation. She wanted him more than she'd ever wanted anything in her entire life.

They had agreed that was not going to happen, and she'd had every intention of sticking to it.

What frightened her, what rocked to her core, was that she was no longer sure there was any way to hold herself back.

10

THE POLICE ARRIVED, questions were asked, statements were taken, and it didn't cool her jets one bit. She sat off in a corner, drinking glass after glass of iced tea and lemonade that the restaurant kept supplying her with, not really noticing how many glasses it was, her eyes glued to Sean, just watching him.

She analyzed this attraction, the compulsion, from every side, dissected it and put it back together. Yes, she wanted him. And she had a pretty good idea he wanted her back.

But her life had no direction at the moment, and his was rooted in Chicago. She had no job and needed to explore new options; he was tied to his and didn't want to change. She had one big (or extremely small) piece of baggage that was number one on her priority list, and nothing, not even a real-live hero with dazzling blue eyes and abs to die for, could change that. She could never ask him to take over and be the daddy to another man's baby, and she could never let any man into her life now if he couldn't be the daddy. Catch-22.

Any way she analyzed it, they were wrong together. The True Blue cop and the shallow media princess, the private man and the public star, the bachelor who kept resisting his mother's attempts to pair him off and the recently engaged woman who came complete with ready-made family on board. It just didn't work. Those pieces did not fit.

But the fact remained: she wanted him. It was there with every breath, every sigh, every move, every heartbeat. She wanted him. To touch, to please, to play with, to tease, to tantalize, to taste, to drive crazy, to be driven crazy by, to have, to hold, to have again... She had played out a whole lot of possibilities and positions in her brain before the saga of the pizza robbery was disposed of by the proper authorities.

Finally, after the suspect had been carted away, they'd taken statements from everyone in the place but her, Sean was debriefed up one side and down the other, a photographer from the newspaper made him pose for pictures with the manager of the restaurant, and everybody around thanked him profusely a few more times, Abra got her chance with him.

When he came to reclaim her, she didn't say a word, just jumped up and hugged him really hard for about ten minutes. At the end of it, she said simply, "You were unbelievable. Unbelievable."

"It was no big deal." But he dipped his head, gathered her close, and hugged her right back, and she knew he was not as unaffected as he seemed. He might be a cop descended from a long line of cops, but ramming people's heads into cash registers and breaking up robberies still wasn't part of his everyday routine. "I'm just glad you're okay."

"Oh, Sean. I was safe under a table, remember? You're the one who went one-on-one with the gun."

He waved a hand, indicating that was a minor inconvenience. "Honestly, Abra, it was nothing. I was just scared because you were there. You never know what can happen. And I wasn't sure you would stay out of the way. Remember, I know you." Shuddering, he closed his eyes for a second. "I thought I was going to have a heart attack when I saw you standing there all woozy, holding that gun, looking like you might just crumple in front of my eyes."

If she hadn't already been totally smitten, his concern for her when he was the one in danger would've put her over the top. "I was fine. Really. I am fine." Brushing his hair off his forehead, she dusted a tiny kiss across the furrows in his brow. "You are so sweet to be worried."

"Abra, you're pregnant. How could I not worry when you were in the same room as a gunman?"

"Let's not talk about it anymore, okay? I'd kind of like to get out of here," she offered. "Ready to go? I don't know if we've been in this place for twelve hours or it just seems that way."

She was hoping to go somewhere more intimate as soon as possible, so she could show him just how grateful she was. If he was amenable, that was. Would he be willing? Was he as stirred and aroused by tonight's events as she was?

She shivered with the deep need that was so much a part of her now, she wasn't sure she would recognize herself without it. If he wasn't willing to satisfy that need tonight, as quickly as possible, she feared she might not survive.

"Let's go," he said, drawing her hand up to his lips and giving her the briefest of kisses. "I'm ready."

Now if she only knew what he was ready for. She couldn't just come out and ask if he wanted to go home and make mad, passionate love the minute they hit the inside of the door. Especially not after she'd made him promise not to make love to her at all.

Major miscalculation on her part. How did she get over this threshold she'd created? Would grabbing him by the front of his sexy black T-shirt and kissing him senseless do it? Maybe she should rip his clothes to shreds and act all wild and wicked? Not exactly her style, but she could improvise.

How about if she peeled off *her* clothes instead, and performed a nice little striptease for him? Would that put him on the road to no return? It wasn't as if she'd ever done anything like that before, but if it came with a guarantee that she'd get lovemaking at the end of it, she was willing to try.

Ply him with liquor? Promise him it was just a one-night stand with no repercussions for anyone? Promise him it was much more than a one-night stand and she would be his forever? Vice versa? All of the above?

It was maddening. If only there was some guarantee that whatever they did, however crazy it became, he would still be her hero, her confidant, her protector tomorrow. If she lost that…she just might die.

With her hand clasped firmly inside his, he led her to the door at a brisk pace. Her legs felt a little wobbly, and she had to concentrate not to stumble.

"Come back any time," the manager called out, running after them to press a large box with a new pizza in it into Sean's hands. "Any time you want to come in, you're welcome. We'll have lifetime free food here for you, okay?"

"Okay," Sean responded with a smile. "My girlfriend loves your pizza, so I think we'll take you up on that."

"Great." He clapped Sean on the shoulder. "Thanks again."

"No problem. Really." To Abra, Sean whispered, "Don't get any ideas. You are not going to be back here every night chowing down on free pizza. Once a week, max."

But her heart was doing a tiny tapdance. He'd just called her his girlfriend. She was sure it didn't mean anything. Just part of whatever explanation he'd given for their appearance at the restaurant. *My girlfriend and I were having dinner when all of a sudden I noticed a man with a gun...* Because he couldn't say, *Media star and missing celebrity Abra Holloway and I were having dinner when all of a sudden I noticed a man with a gun...*

"Why didn't they ask me for a statement, Sean?" she inquired, sidling up closer, curling herself around his arm as they walked across the parking lot in the cool night air. She just couldn't stop touching him. Somewhere, somehow, she wanted to be connected. "They talked to everyone else, and I was getting a little worried that I was going to have to either think up a fake name and identity or else throw myself on their mercy. But I figure you worked it out somehow so I didn't have to. What did you tell them?"

"Aw, Abra, you're probably not going to like it. I

told them we were both married to other people, that this was an out-of-town tryst, and I would really appreciate it if they would keep your name out of it." Pulling away slightly, balancing the pizza box, he looked rueful. He also looked gorgeous, all shadows and angles in the dusky light of the parking lot.

An out-of-town tryst. If only. Out-of-town, in-town... She would take any tryst she could get. "That's fine, Sean," she assured him. "Whatever cover story you came up with is fine by me. But they bought that?"

"Sure. Why not?"

"Men." She shook her head. "The old boy network. As long as they think you're cheating on your wife, they'll cover for you. It's kind of disgusting when you think about it."

"I told you you wouldn't like it."

"You think you're so smart. How is it you know me so well, anyway?" she mused.

"It's my uncanny knack for the truth," he joked. "Remind me to tell you about that sometime."

"Hmm... Uncanny knack for the truth? That sounds bogus. Especially when you're making up stories about how we're married to other people and cheating on these fictional spouses and..." She shook her head. "Never mind. You got me out of giving a statement, which might've translated to panicking and confessing everything in this case."

"I may not have even needed the out-of-town tryst angle. I also told them you were under the table the whole time and didn't see anything." He pulled his keys out of his pocket, glancing down at them in his palm, halting as they neared his car. "Whichever part they bought, as a courtesy for a fellow cop, they looked the other way."

"But you know I saw the whole thing?"

"Yes."

"And I touched the gun." Even as she said it out loud, she couldn't believe it. "Oh, my god, Sean! I was holding the gun. Isn't that important? Plus my fingerprints are probably on it!"

"I wiped it."

He said it so matter-of-factly. "You wiped off my fingerprints? So you're saying that you out-and-out lied to fellow police officers and screwed around with evidence?"

"Yes."

"Just to keep me incognito?"

"Yes."

"Oh, God, Sean." Tipping back her head, wondering how she'd gotten to a place where she was actually glad that a stand-up, moral guy had compromised his principles on her behalf, she stared up at the stars far above them. Here she'd been thinking of seducing him for her own evil pleasure, and he was saving her life, foiling robberies, compromising his principles, and probably leaping tall buildings in a single bound while he was at it. "This is all so unfair to you."

He bent to stick the pizza box in the back seat, but edged back around to send her a speculative gaze. "Maybe I should be the one who decides what's fair to me."

"You can cut me all the slack you want, but it's still

not fair to you, however you slice it," she insisted, awash in guilt. "You lied for me. That has to be eating at you."

"Everybody lies," he whispered.

Leaning back against the car, he reached for her, tipping her closer with one swift motion. Whoosh. One minute she was safe on her own side, torn and conflicted about pushing him further than he wanted to go, and the next, before she even had time to react, she was in over her head again. He braced himself, edging apart his muscular thighs just enough to fit her up against the length of his body, his hands firmly planted at the small of her back, holding her there securely, while he dipped his head to greedily nuzzle her neck.

Surprised at how fast he'd managed to maneuver them into this, Abra sucked in her breath. Her sundress, a little white piece of cotton with tiny flowers scattered on it, gapped in the front where she was slammed up hard against him. It wasn't an expensive dress, far from it, but she'd chosen it because it was fitted in the bodice and cut more roomy in the waist and hips, which fit her newly expanding body. Since all of her bras were too small at the moment, it was also a big plus that this dress didn't need one.

When she'd tried it on, the rise of bosom showing at the neckline had made her feel sexy and flirty. But now... There was so much pale skin, so much cleavage, overflowing into his chest. That wasn't just flirtatious, it was positively lewd. She'd never had a bosom like this before, so she hadn't been aware this kind of thing could happen. Right now, glancing down, she was a little worried she was going to pop right out of the inadequate dress.

And the hard buds of her nipples rose up on cue, too, eager in the cool night air, way too obvious behind the thin white fabric. If she did overflow her dress, she'd be bare-breasted and bare-legged in a parking lot in the middle of Campustown, her hair all rumpled, her makeup smeared, wearing plastic flip-flops and a cheap white cotton dress off-the-rack at WalMart.

The Abra Holloway she used to be would've turned up her nose at the dress, let alone this kind of lascivious display in a parking lot. This one didn't care who saw her or what was polite. She didn't want to wait to get in the car. She just wanted to feel him around her right here, right now. If her breasts spilled out, so be it.

Tousled, wanton, on fire, she closed her eyes, her body humming as his lips slid down the slope of her neck. Her hands tangled behind his head, urging him on, as she sighed with the pure bliss of it, rubbing her cheek against his. If he didn't get to her mouth soon, she wouldn't be responsible for her actions.

After waiting so long, biding her time with iced tea and soft drinks until she thought she might float, watching him and wanting him for hours, she could feel the sensations building, beginning where his lips and his hands touched her, rippling through the rest of her body, toppling one over the other. It didn't take much to flip her switches. Her breasts, her thighs, deep in her core, she was one big shiver.

He turned at that second, bracketing her face with

his beautiful hands, covering her mouth with his, plunging his tongue inside to meet hers. She moaned her pleasure into his mouth. She had never felt so complete. And they were just getting started.

Just then bright light flashed in the periphery of her vision. "Am I seeing stars?" she murmured.

Sean went still. "No. You're seeing a flash," he said roughly.

"What?"

But he had already tugged up her dress up in the front and set her neatly aside, leaving her bereft and alone next to the car. He took off, sprinting past three parked cars, going after a man in a strange khaki vest who was trying to run in the opposite direction. She recognized that vest. He was the newspaper photographer who had snapped Sean inside. With one hand across the front of her bodice to hide whatever needed to be hidden, she shaded her eyes from the glare of the parking lot lights, trying to see what was happening.

"Give me the camera," Sean yelled.

No response from the other guy. He kept running. "Oof" was all she heard as Sean knocked him down. There was a scuffle, followed by the man shouting, "Damn it, I think you broke my zoom!" as Sean punched him one and then snatched a camera away from him. Then he stalked back toward her, looking like a study in banked rage, as the photographer scrambled to his feet.

The man in the vest dusted off his clothes and patted down his pockets, protesting, "Aw, come on! Why can't I take a picture of a cute couple canoo-

dling? I can already tell you the cutline: Hero Enjoys
A Private Reward After Foiling Robbery. It'll look
great in the paper."

"It was supposed to be a *private* moment," Sean
shot back. "Not for publication."

"Right now, you qualify as breaking news, buddy.
Your privacy doesn't matter when you're news." He
yelled, "You'd better give it back. I can sue you.
You're stealing my property."

"Go right ahead and sue." Sean looked like he was
going to shove the camera in the car, but he changed
his mind at the last moment. Instead, he opened the
back, spooled out the whole roll of film, flung it
around in a wide arc until he was sure it was beyond
repair, and then tossed the camera back to its owner.
"You can have it back now. So you can't accuse me of
stealing it, can you?"

Abra was sort of frightened of him in this new, angry incarnation. Impressed, glad he was on her side,
incredibly turned on, and frightened, all at the same
time. She had her door shut and locked before Sean
had the key in the ignition. "Can you be arrested for
knocking him down?"

"Maybe. Probably not."

Risking even more for her. Her bill just kept running higher and higher. "Can we get out of here?"
she pleaded. "The faster, the better."

Outside, the photographer pounded on Sean's window and kicked at the side of his car. Sean ignored
him, putting it in Reverse, speeding out onto the
street. Back in the lot, another flash lit up the space.

Abra craned her neck to see what was going on. "Why would he use his flash again?"

"I don't know. Maybe he had another roll of film hidden in one of the pockets on his vest and he took a shot of my departing license plate. Who cares?" His expression was hard and implacable, and he stared straight ahead out the windshield. "Look, I'm sorry I tackled the guy. I know the last thing you needed was another altercation tonight."

"Are you kidding?" She scooted sideways to face him. "First the robbery and now this. I've never had anyone get into fights just to protect me. The adrenaline is amazing."

"Is that good?"

"Do you really have to ask?" Her jaw dropped. He didn't know? He didn't know that she was so overloaded from pining for him that she could barely stand up? Not to mention the fact that he had saved her bacon at least twice tonight, lying and stealing to keep her from being exposed. How could he not know how much that meant to her? She was speechless.

"I'm asking. Tell me."

Since she was basically a chicken, Abra went with the easy part first. "I don't know how much of either of us was visible or identifiable in those photos, but if they had run, if anyone had said, gee, that looks like Abra Holloway with bad hair, it could've been awful. Game over. You saved it, Sean. You saved me. Again."

"So it's all about playing hide-and-seek then? You're grateful I'm helping you stay hidden?"

"No!" she exploded. "That's the least of it. Oh, my God, Sean, you're making me nuts. How can you not know what you do to me?"

His voice was husky when he said, "Tell me."

"Tell you? About how my brain and my body react to you in full-blown protector mode? Is it good for me? Oh, yeeaaaah." Sinking into her seat, she drew out the word, giving it a shivery, shaky sound to approximate the way she felt inside. "Oh, baby, it is the very definition of good."

He tore his eyes away from the road to stare at her as if he were hypnotized. Either that or horrified. "What are you saying?"

"That I want you, you moron!" She had never seen anything as gorgeous or as *hot* as Sean Calhoun when he got rolling. She was so frustrated, so beyond being able to control what she said or did. She needed him to know why. "I know we said this wouldn't and couldn't happen, but I am past the point where I can stop it. I want you, Sean. I need you. I need to feel you with me." She swallowed. "Making love to me. Making love with me. I want every bit of what that entails."

His groan was audible. "Abra, I'm so close to smashing the hell out of the promise I made to you," he warned. "The one about not making love to you. True Blue be damned. I'm human, you know. You need to pull back now if there is even a shadow of a doubt that you'll be sorry later."

"I want it," she rushed to say, her pulse pounding. She abandoned her side of the seat and slid over onto his, demonstrating her fervent desire not to pull back.

"I want *you*, Sean." Cozying up next to him, she whispered, "I think I love you."

Uh-oh. The L-word had leapt out of nowhere, right into the open. The idea of it made her chest tight and her knees weak. But she couldn't even try to stop the confessions around him anymore. He already knew her deepest secrets. Except there was this new one. The one with the L-word in it.

"I can't deal with this right now." He looked like he might start banging his head against the wheel any second.

"But you don't have to deal with it now," she continued. "I'm fine with it if you don't love me back. Really. Because I *know* I love you."

His blue eyes were a smoky gray when he glanced her way. "You think I don't love you back? Abra, I am so in love with you I can't even breathe anymore. That's not the issue. The issue is what happens once we know that. What do we do with it? I want you. But you better be damn sure we're doing the right thing if we take the leap. There's a lot at stake here."

Abra, I am so in love with you I can't even breathe anymore. She knew it! Relief and joy swept over her.

"This could be something really wonderful, you know that, right?" she asked him. She brushed his cheek with her finger, overcome with tenderness. "This love thing is kind of new to me. So if there's lust mixed in here—and there definitely is—oh, wow, is there lust—I want you to know that I have real feelings for you, too."

He smiled, and even that small motion, as his cheek curved into the smile under her hand, was enough to make her quiver deep inside. She tilted her head onto his shoulder, drinking him in.

"These are the real, true, abiding kind of feelings," she mused, gaining confidence as she thought it through. "The kind you have when you want to spend all day and all night making love to someone until you're so tired you can't even sit up, and then a few more days and nights doing crossword puzzles and watching old movies and *not* making love, because you need to build your stamina back up." Laughing, bewildered, she murmured, "I don't know where this is coming from. I've never done that. I don't think I've ever felt this way before."

"I hope not. You sound pretty crazy, Abra." He sent her a dubious, almost fearful look and stuck his hand on her forehead. "You sure you're feeling okay? This isn't some kind of delayed shock, is it?"

"Of course not." She batted his hand off her head. "I've been thinking about this for days. It's just that I'm finally brave enough—or maybe insane enough—to tell you about it." Her words tumbled over each other. She just couldn't seem to get them out fast enough. "You know what you said about there being a lot at stake for the two of us? See, that's why I've been holding this all back and why it's all kind of blowing up now."

"I just don't want you to regret it later, that's all."

"I know. Because there's the rest of our lives to consider. We really need to get some sex out of the way, under our belts, now, so we can concentrate on the rest of our lives later." That sounded so bizarre, she started to laugh. "There's my sanity to consider, too, you know. I might just lose what's left of my mind if you don't get your clothes off and start making love to me within the next five minutes."

"Abra—"

She ignored him, working up some enthusiasm for this project. He didn't seem to be nearly as aroused or insatiable as she was. How fair was that? Mischievously, she whispered, "I might just melt into a puddle on the seat if you don't get me home within those five minutes, Sean. And then, just as soon as we hit the front door, you're going to have to make love to me for about six hours."

"Abra—"

"No, don't stop me." All the pent-up feelings from today—all the pent-up feelings of the past few days, of knocking around that tiny house, tripping over Sean and his beautiful body parts—fueled her higher. She knew she was out of control, she wasn't playing fair, and she might just get them both into a car wreck. She didn't care.

"I might not be able to wait the five minutes to get home," she murmured into his ear, touching her tongue to his lobe, enjoying the way he flinched and ground his teeth. She tipped closer, letting the straps of her dress slide over her shoulders as she rubbed her breasts into the side of his arm.

He tried to hold her off with that hand, driving with the left one. "Abra—"

Into his ear, she breathed, "I might just have to rip off your clothes, strip off my dress, and see what kind of gymnastics we can get up to right here in the car." She reached for the edge of his black T-shirt, balling it into her fist, skating closer to the top button on his jeans. "I might just have to unzip—"

"Stop, Abra," he said ferociously. "Stop. If you don't shut up, keep your clothes on, and get back on your own side, I'll pull over right now and we'll just see who wins the war on vehicular mischief."

"Who's stopping you?"

He shot her a blazing look, and then he hit the gas. Hard.

She smiled in triumph, sitting back in her seat, counting the seconds. One-two-three... By her estimate, they were in her driveway in under two minutes.

He shut off the ignition. He unbuckled his seat belt and flung it out the way. And then he lunged.

11

"SEE WHAT HAPPENS WHEN you play with fire?" he growled.

"Bring it," she challenged, but it was too late. He already had.

Before she had time to take a deep breath, he had flipped her flat on her back, using his left hand to pin her hands over her head up by the door handle. As she lay there, panting, wondering how he did that, he pulled back enough to survey her up and down with this wicked light in his eyes.

"You seem to be at a disadvantage," he drawled. "Guess we get to play this my way."

That was one way of putting it. With her dress scrunched up around her hips and dipping low on the top, with her hands trapped over her head, giving her more cleavage than any Wonderbra, she wasn't just at a disadvantage, she was toast. This was not how she had foreseen her seduction scene. He was supposed to be putty in her hands, not vice versa.

Every time she took a breath, her breasts pushed against the tight bodice, aching to be freed. Sean's eyes seemed glued there for a long moment.

One plastic flip-flop was gone, while the other one was stuck partially underneath her. It was uncomfortable under there, and she wiggled a little to try to get it to fall off the seat, but that just bunched up more folds of her dress at her waist. Sean took that as an invitation to slide his right hand down there and dispose of the shoe, but also to explore all the bare skin that was now visible. Everything from her belly button down was fair game.

It was hot inside the car, and the window over her head was beginning to steam over. Abra closed her eyes and leaned backward, quivering with anticipation as he tested the lace edge of her bikini panties with one finger. Arching her hips up off the seat, she tried to telegraph to him that he could strip off her panties and be done with them right now and that would suit her just fine. She was so wet, so ready to get to the part where his skin met her skin. She had been ready for days.

But he didn't. He drew the panties down an inch or two over her hips, but then left them there. Instead he scooped her bottom in his palm, squeezing gently, creating more ripples of sensation, before skating his finger to tease the inside of her thigh.

"Ohh. Sean..." This was so unfair. She wanted to be torturing *him* and driving *him* crazy. Instead, she was practically naked, whimpering under him, letting him play her like a harp, while he was fully clothed and completely in control.

He was hardly touching her, just dancing around on her bare skin, trailing sparks from one hot spot to the next, but not stopping long enough to put out any fires. In fact, he seemed to purposely move on just when things were getting good. He was toying with her. *Toying* with her.

"Are you trying to make me beg?" she demanded, attempting to sit up, or at least drag a leg around him and pull his hips down.

His eyes were heavy-lidded, but he was still smiling that crooked half smile. "That a fantasy of yours? To beg?"

Damn insufferable man. "No, it's a fantasy of mine to make you beg." Wrenching her hands free, she took him by surprise, sitting up, tangling her arms around his neck, slamming her mouth into his and shoving him backward into the steering wheel.

Now, with her in his lap and in control, things were going to get good. She lifted herself into his warm, delicious mouth, using the distraction of the kiss to snake a hand down and reach for the metal rivet at the top of his jeans.

"No," he said, grabbing her wrist and holding it away from his pants.

"No?"

"No." Letting go of her hand, he began to drop small, soft kisses in the corners of her lips, on her throat and her cheeks, one at a time, with painstaking care. "What's your rush?"

"Rush is good," she murmured, tipping her head back and giving in to the heavenly feel of those small caresses. "Rush means not thinking, just doing. That's what I want." She immediately shifted her hands back to his pants.

"I want the thinking," he said darkly. "I want your head in the bed, too, not just your body. And I sure don't want our first time to be fast, crazy sex in the damn car."

"But—"

"I know I was playing along, but that was just to see how far you'd go." He swore under his breath. "But for real, Abra, for our first time, I want it slow. In the bed. Me, you, all the time in the world. Let's go inside and do it right."

"We can do that later," she promised. "But now, let's just do this my way." She had her hand on his fly again before he could stop her.

"No."

"C'mon, Sean," she said huskily, getting the zipper down an inch or two. "You know you're as turned on as I am."

"Don't push me, Abra." His expression was fierce as he dumped her unceremoniously out of his lap and refastened his pants. "I'm getting the feeling this is all about sex for you, or maybe getting your way. I want more than that. If I didn't..."

Frustrated, he let out a particularly pithy curse as he ran his hand through his hair. "If it's all about who's in charge, we both know I can end that debate in about three seconds. That's about how long it would take me to flip you over onto your stomach and cuff your hands behind your back."

"Game over," she whispered. Her mouth went dry. That sounded pretty dandy to her, handcuffs and all. She couldn't fight when he had all the weapons. "Okay."

He blinked. "Okay, what?"

"Okay. Whatever you want. Wherever. Just don't make me beg."

"Oh, Abra..." He slanted his mouth across hers,

kissing her deeper and sweeter, and she couldn't resist that kind of invitation.

Shoving her hands into his soft, golden brown hair, she opened her mouth wider, sliding her tongue over his, surrendering. However he wanted it, that was the way she wanted it, too. For now.

"But we are going to come back here and try it with the cuffs," she promised. "You don't just put an idea like that in my head and never deliver."

"Now you know how I feel about the kitchen table."

Abra's eyes danced. "So we'll get to both the handcuffs in the car and the kitchen table in due time. Good. We can make a list. I like lists."

She could feel his smile against her own before he kissed her again, quick, and then slid backward, fooled with the handle, and let himself out of the car. As he bent back in the door, he extended a hand. "Let's go inside."

Barefoot, half-dressed, she couldn't get out of that car fast enough.

It was a race to see who could get to the door, who could get to the key, who could get to the bedroom. But then they both stopped and slowed.

Sean found some candles in the kitchen and brought them into the bedroom as she turned back the covers to reveal her favorite Egyptian-cotton sheets, the ones she'd brought with her from New York. Once he lit the candles, he dimmed the lights, and her heart turned over at how pretty the room looked. So romantic. He was right. The car was fun and frantic, reckless and sexy in a crazy way, but this was different. More deliberate. More important somehow.

Uh-oh. How important was this? Would they find out new things during that would affect them after? How could they not?

Her heart began to thud. She was thinking again. Bad things always happened when she started thinking.

But he took her hand and raised it to his lips, and once again, she found herself melting. It was just so easy for him to turn her on and off, to make himself irresistible and put everything else out of her mind.

"I, uh, said we would do this however you want, Sean. Your rules. Your timetable." Almost shyly, she lifted her gaze. "So how would that be?"

"Like this." His arms were around her, strong and hard, his lips were nuzzling her neck, and his hands moved to the zipper at the back of her dress. "Let's get you out of this and into something more comfortable. Like the bed."

He slipped the straps over her shoulders, letting the fabric slide off her body and pool around her ankles. For once in her life, Abra wasn't worried about how she looked. She stood there, letting him gaze as long as he wanted. They'd both waited forever for this moment, so they might as well make it last.

"Wow," he whispered. "You are the most beautiful woman I have ever seen."

In her profession, people told her she was beautiful way too often, but it was all about the outside, about the new Gucci suit or the old Chanel gown. Somehow, in Sean's eyes, she knew it was more than that.

How funny that she'd had to gain ten pounds, dye her hair, buy cheap clothes and lose her makeup to feel really beautiful in his eyes.

She smiled at him. It was surprisingly provocative just to stand there and try to be patient as his eyes flickered over her body. She bit her lip, doing her best not to move. But her breasts felt so heavy, so full, and her nipples tightened and peaked under his gaze.

If something didn't happen soon, she might just come apart at the seams, right in front of him. She was not a woman for whom orgasms came all that easily. But tonight...it wasn't going to take much.

Abra broke first. After all, it wasn't fair for her to be wearing nothing but a pair of bikini pants and him distinctly overdressed. "Let's get you out of this," she said softly, reaching to strip his T-shirt over his head. "And into something more comfortable." She paused. "Like me."

His sharp intake of air was gratifying.

With a gentle shove, he toppled her backward, right onto the bed. She couldn't help a small giggle, but it was choked off in her throat when he stripped off his jeans and his tighty whities in one fluid motion and slipped onto the bed beside her.

"I have never seen a more beautiful man," she whispered, drinking him in with her eyes. In the shadow of the candlelight, his skin looked golden. Beautiful. She set her palm on his smooth, warm, muscled chest, feeling his heart beat under her hand, wondering how she'd gotten so lucky as to be in this bed with this man at this time. "Wow. Just...wow."

"My feelings exactly."

Running her hand down to his hip, she took her time, getting the feel of him, marveling at the way his body was so different from hers. Fascinated, really taking the time to explore him in a way she'd never done with a man before, Abra brushed her lips over the hard plane of his hip and the sharp angles of his washboard abs, running her tongue into every little byway. He groaned as she started to head a little farther south.

"Not yet," he said in a rough voice.

Instead, he pulled her up against him, legs tangled together, thigh over thigh, his flat stomach pressed to her softer one, his erection hard and insistent between them. He was holding back, barely grazing the front of her silk panties, but she felt the pulse deep within her. His hands framed her face as he kissed her, long, slow, unbearably sweet. She adored his kisses, but it wasn't nearly enough. Not nearly.

One hand moved to her breast, following the curve, tweaking her nipple, and she let out a long "oooh" sound without realizing she'd even opened her mouth. He backed off immediately.

"Did it hurt?" he asked.

"Oh, no. It's wonderful." She set his hand right back where it was. Her voice caught when she said, "They're just really sensitive right now, and you don't know how good that feels. I have been dying for exactly that, Sean. Just don't stop."

When his mouth and tongue followed where his hand had been, giving exquisite care to one breast and then the other, she thought she truly might die. She could also feel tremors starting to pool below her belly. What? He hadn't even touched her down there, and she was climbing toward the sky. When he moved to kiss her full on the mouth again, deeper, harder, his hand still on her breast, pinching her pebbled nipple just a tiny bit, things started to get very shaky.

She let out a little gasp and grabbed a handful of sheet, angling closer, rubbing herself against him, moaning as waves of pleasure radiated from that one spot where her center now met his rigid length. With his free hand cupping her bottom, keeping her pressed exactly where she needed to be, she toppled over the edge so hard and so fast her brain couldn't quite keep up. He wasn't letting go; he wouldn't let her stop or pause or wait.

"Ooooooh," she shuddered, shattering into a million pieces as she held on to Sean for dear life. Amazing.

As the waves receded, she gasped for breath. Weakly, she murmured, "I have never felt anything like that before. Oh, my God."

He tipped his forehead against hers, breathing almost as hard as she was. "Watching you, that was incredible."

Now when she wrapped her hand around him, stroking his hardness, he didn't stop her. He did reach over to peel off her panties, and she knew what was coming next.

Finally. The consummation, the connection she had been waiting for. Relief.

But...

Pulling away, she placed her hand over his. "Before we..." She stopped, not sure what to say.

"What?" he asked. "You don't want to?"

"No, I do want to. It's just." Oh, jeez. What a terrible time for her brain to kick back in. "Sean, in the heat of the moment in the car, I kind of didn't think about some things, but now that we're taking this a little slower, with more thinking..."

"Oh, hell." He groaned as he lay back on the pillow. "I was the one who wanted you to be thinking in bed, wasn't I?"

"Yes, but that's okay. I mean, normally I would agree with you that I tend to overthink things, but at this particular time, well, it may be good to be forewarned," she began.

He picked up his head. "Forewarned? About what? I have a condom if that's it."

Distracted, she demanded, "Why would you have a condom? I thought you thought we weren't going to do this?"

"I'm not stupid, Abra. I knew when I promised you there was a certain chance... Never mind." He pulled the pillow over head, but she yanked it right back off again.

"No, I want to know."

"When I got you the glasses you never wore. I picked up some condoms. Just in case. There's one on the nightstand," he told her. "I was going to get to that before we went any further. So if that was what you were worried about..."

"No. Not at all." She sat up, clutching the sheet to her chin. "I just wanted to warn you...about me...

You see, I did check out the part of the pregnancy book about... Well, about this."

"The pregnancy book covers sex?" he asked, clearly surprised.

"Yes. Because people have questions as to whether they can or can't," she said plainly. "It's very normal to have questions, especially if your hormones are telling you that you want it 24/7."

"Please don't tell me that we got this far and now you're going to say it's off-limits. Because..." Sean sat up, too, but he put his arm around her, patting her shoulder. "No, never mind," he said with conviction. "If we shouldn't do one specific thing, I'm sure there are others we can do. We'll make it work. I'm creative."

"Oh, no, we can," she assured him. "I mean, the book says that unless your doctor says no, and especially this early in the pregnancy, there shouldn't be any reason why not. It's just that..."

"What?" he demanded. "What?"

Why had she brought this up. Just when what she wanted was so close to her grasp. Why?

He clenched his jaw. "Abra, tell me now," he ordered her.

"Things may feel different," she whispered.

"Different? What do you mean?"

"The book says it may be—" she held her breath "—tight. And wet."

Sean bit down on his lip so hard she could see blood. "Abra," he managed after a moment, "tight and wet are very good things."

"Yes, but—"

"No. No more. It will be fine." He kissed her forehead, quickly, with the merest brush of his lips. "You just tell me what you need and what you like, and we'll be fine."

"What I need is you inside me. What I like is you inside me." She set her hand on his bare chest, shocked that the arc of electricity hummed through like always. They were naked, she'd had a mind-blowing climax, they had a really stupid discussion, and yet, the erotic connection was still there.

"I can do that," he said. He reached for the condom on the nightstand, but she got there first.

"Let me." She opened the foil packet with her teeth, removing it carefully, concentrating on what she needed to do. So what if her hands were shaking? She could figure it out.

It took a second, and she felt really stupid, but Sean seemed to be, um, fine. Better than fine. That was impressive. When it was done, pleased with her handiwork, and even more pleased that he hadn't laughed at her, she slid herself up his body. His eyes were that smoky gray-blue again, and she started to feel the shivers as she clambered on top of him.

Underneath her, Sean was one firm, unyielding surface. Easy to brace herself, to straddle his hips, to tip over and kiss his chest, find just the right place, and then to slip right down and take him inside.

The pleasure was so intense, she had to close her eyes and hold herself very still. But he was moving under her, stroking up and in, and there was no holding back.

It was...bliss. She was with Sean every second,

watching his eyes and his expressions, knowing for the first time in her life that she was where she belonged. With him.

And when she felt the shivers begin again, when Sean began to lose himself as well, it seemed inevitable. Right. Perfect.

As they rose and fell together in one astonishing sweep of passion, as she crashed onto his chest, she whispered, "I love you, Sean. This was perfect."

"Perfect," he echoed, reeling her in, holding her close.

"Sean?"

He lifted his head. "Yeah?"

She didn't want to break the mood, but her mind was racing again... "Do you think that babies get freaked out when their parents are kind of hot for each other?" she asked awkwardly. "I mean, it's good exercise, so in that way, it's good for the baby. But it must be kind of strange sitting in there listening to all the ruckus."

His laughter was muffled by the pillow as he turned over and dropped a kiss on her lips. "No, Abra. I think our baby will know it's all part of the process. It's good. It means Mom and Dad are in love."

"Oh." She swallowed. This was what happened when she was utterly satisfied and completely relaxed. She got careless. She'd just inadvertently referred to them as the baby's parents, and then he'd said our baby. *Our* baby. Mom and Dad. Was that what they were now?

Somehow, without her even noticing, they had slid

into a definite relationship. It was sweet and sexy and honest and everything she could ever have wanted. But very, very scary.

SHE HAD NO IDEA WHAT time it was when she drifted awake. Content, peaceful, steady as a rock... At first she thought she was dreaming. She'd had so many fantasies about Sean and beds that actually waking up in one with him didn't seem real. But there he was, sleeping serenely, just as gorgeous first thing in the morning as he was in the wee hours of night.

Abra smiled and cuddled in closer, thinking maybe he would be amenable to another romp or two this morning. If it was still morning. She squinted at the clock. Well, just barely.

She hadn't been sleeping well at all, and certainly not this late. "I guess we wore each other out," she said under her breath. But what a way to go.

"You awake?" Sean lifted his head far enough to send her a sleepy stare. "What time is it?"

"After eleven. But don't worry. We don't have anything to do today but... Whatever we want." Like lounge around and make love. She hoped. She laid her head back down on the pillow so she could stare at him some more. "Unless you have plans."

"Well, there is the kitchen table. It's on my short-list."

Abra could feel herself blushing. After last night, she couldn't believe she still had the capacity to blush. He was probably going to bring up handcuffs and the car next, and she really would have to die of shame.

"That can wait," she mumbled. She scrambled out the other side of the bed, rustling around till she found her orange sweat pants and the matching tank top. She put them on with all due haste. "I, uh, I'm going to make you some breakfast, Sean. You sleep in."

As she poked through the refrigerator, trying to scrape up something that remotely resembled breakfast, she heard the water running in the shower. That would probably kill breakfast in bed, but maybe she could convince him to jump back in again so she could serve him. If she could cook anything in the first place. Which was a big if.

Feeling quite industrious, she found a tray, an egg, bread for toast, and she even started the coffeemaker. This was all a major accomplishment. She hadn't actually cracked the egg yet when she heard a phone ringing. There was no phone in the house—she'd never turned on any kind of service, because who did she have to call?—and her cell phone had run out of power the last time she'd called for pizza. So she knew it must be Sean's, the one in his back pocket she'd used to call 911.

"Sean?" she tried, traipsing back to the bedroom. But the water was still running. "Sean," she shouted at the bathroom, "your pants are ringing."

Should she answer? What if it was important?

She opened it up and tried to figure out how to answer it. But it was very small, and there was no button that said "ANS" on it or anything like that. She did, however, see a red button, a blue button, and a green button. The green one was what she'd used last night at the restaurant to call out, so that wasn't right. What about the blue one?

She tried it. Cradling the tiny phone to her ear, she heard "Message One" and a date and time that indicated the call had come in earlier that week.

It was probably not nice to listen to his messages, but she could tell the voice was his mother, and she was curious what she sounded like. Besides, she and Sean had no secrets from each other, right?

"Where are you, hon?" Mrs. Calhoun asked several times, getting increasingly impatient. "I keep trying to get ahold of you and you never answer. Get with the program, Sean."

There was even one where she demanded to know if he'd found the "cheap piece of Christmas trash" yet and if not, why not.

"Cheap piece of Christmas trash?" Abra repeated. She liked his mother's voice—she sounded like a real spitfire—but she didn't like that bit about cheap Christmas trash. She sniffed, "I can't believe he thought that could be me."

The last one had just come in yesterday. "Hon, it's Mom again. I just wanted you to know that Cooper may've found the tootsie so you can come home. I don't know if that's good news or bad, but there you are. Oh, and your friend Bill called this afternoon and said that no, there's no APB out on Abra Holloway but if you know where she is, you can probably make some serious bucks off it."

Abra heard her own name, and felt a sudden chill in the room. In her ear, Sean's mother's voice said, "Isn't she that girl on TV? What's that all about, hon?

I didn't know you knew her. Oh, and Bill seemed to think I told you to find out about her. I don't get that."

The words coming out of the cell phone were just a blur at this point. "That's it. Well, anyway, call me soon. I'm worried about you, Sean. Come home!"

The phone dangled from Abra's hand, beeping to signal there were no more messages.

But she was still in shock. He was asking about APBs and telling some guy named Bill to run background checks? Sure, he'd slept with her. He'd shared every inch of his body with her. He even said he loved her. *Abra, I am so in love with you I can't even breathe anymore.* But he had to do a little background check first, didn't he?

She had worked herself up to a good head of steam by the time he emerged from the shower. "Sean," she said in a very clipped tone, paying no attention to the fact that he was only wearing a towel. And he looked wet. And shiny. And amazing. No, she didn't notice any of that. Balling her hands into fists, she felt like she was going to cry. "Sean, your phone rang."

"So?"

"So I made the mistake of trying to answer it, but I got your messages instead."

"And you heard my mother's voice a hundred times?" he asked warily. "So?"

"Did you tell some Bill person that you knew where I was?" she inquired coldly. "Did you? Should I be expecting the Chicago PD to be breaking down the door later today?"

"Of course not," he returned, stung. "I needed to

know if I was breaking the law by helping you stay hidden. You can understand how that might be a problem for a police officer, right? But I didn't say anything about where you were. I just asked if there was any kind of search for you, by the authorities, that I needed to know about."

"Oh, come on. You're happy to lie and obstruct justice when you feel like it," she snapped. "Why couldn't you do what I wanted? Why couldn't you see that you telling your friend to look for information on me could be very dangerous?"

"Abra, sweetheart, don't get upset," he said in his most soothing voice. He came around behind her and wrapped his arms around her. "Nothing has happened. Nothing is going to happen. It's not good for you to get stressed and there's no reason to."

Maybe he was right. Maybe she was just overreacting. After all, this was True Blue Sean she was talking about. He wouldn't endanger her. "It was just so weird knowing you'd been talking to someone else about me," she muttered. "Plus my emotions are all over the map. I guess I don't trust my feelings anymore."

"But you can trust me," he assured her. "You know that."

Securely inside his embrace, she did know that. "Last night was so good, I don't want to screw it up, you know? You're the best thing that ever happened to me, Sean. I don't want to mess it up the way I always mess everything up."

"You won't. I won't let you."

She nodded, relaxing into him. "Okay."

"Okay." He spun her around to face him. "How about if we stay in today, just eat Chunky Monkey and leftover pizza and read the newspaper in bed? I can go out and get a paper, so we can see what they said about the robbery."

"I started making breakfast in bed for you, you know. You just got up too soon. I made coffee for you and I don't even drink coffee." She managed a smile as she backed toward the door. "And I do get a newspaper, oddly enough. It's leftover from the professor I'm subletting the house from. So you get back in bed, I'll get the paper and see how the coffee is doing, and then maybe I can get cracking on that egg."

"Just don't poison me," he called after her.

Continuing her internal dialogue, weighing pros and cons and finding lots more pros in her situation with Sean, she was feeling a lot better about the whole Bill and the APB thing when she got to the front door. She had her hand on the knob, she pulled it open, she bent to pick up the paper, and...

All hell broke loose. Bulbs flashed, people started to scream her name, microphones and cameras and news trucks appeared out of nowhere, and the small side street in Urbana began to look like Times Square at midnight.

She whirled back into the house, slamming the door shut. But it was too late. Everyone in the world knew where Abra Holloway had been hiding.

12

IT HAD TO BE A BAD JOKE. Abra's mind was whirling. Who? When? How?

Maybe it was just a nightmare. Not real. Her brain was playing tricks on her. From last night's bliss to this... In one fell swoop? It couldn't be real, could it?

She crept into the living room. Peeking out the curtains, filled with dread, she verified that, no, it was not a fantasy, and yes, there really were all sorts of people out there, milling around, buzzing with the excitement of a major scoop, all desperate to catch another glimpse of her. The creepiest thing was the guy who was right on the other side of the window, apparently trying to peep in. She snatched the drapes together, blocking the light and the view.

What to do? What to do?

Her first thought was to flee, but how? There was nowhere to go. She lifted a hand to her forehead. If they had the front of the house and the street staked out that completely, surely there were more cameras and reporters around the back, too. She was caught like a rat in a trap.

All she could think of was to turn on the television, to check the news programs and see how far the story had traveled. Would they be talking about her? Oh, yes, they would. There was her face on one channel, and she caught her name in the crawl at the bottom of the screen on another. Oh, brother. She was all over the place.

"At the top of the hour, sources in the Midwest report that former media darling and television advice sweetheart Abra Holloway has been located," the CNN anchor intoned, with a headshot of Abra from *The Shelby Show* visible over her shoulder. "We do not have a statement from Holloway yet regarding her disappearance, but witnesses indicate that a few moments ago, she was actually spotted at the home she has apparently been renting in the university town of Urbana, Illinois. Although witnesses at the scene said she appeared somewhat disheveled, she also seems to be in good health."

Abra blinked at the television, stunned. They were already reporting on the fact that she had opened her door just minutes before? It was surreal.

The reporter continued, "Although fans and sponsors were left mystified when Holloway abruptly left the syndicated talk show, *The Shelby Show*, earlier this month, initial information confirms that Holloway is unharmed, and in fact, sources now tell us that she apparently left New York City because of a secret romantic involvement with a Chicago police detective."

"A secret romantic involvement? What the...?" Abra sat down on the sofa with a thump.

"Our sources indicate that the man in the case is one—" the anchorwoman checked a sheaf of papers in front of her "—Sean Calhoun. Further details are unavailable at this time, and we have no response as of yet from Holloway's current fiancé, millionaire entrepreneur Julian Wheelwright. As the story breaks, we hope to have more information for you on this developing story, as well as current photos and perhaps some kind of statement from Holloway herself. CNN reporters are at the site in Urbana, as well as in Chicago to see if we can track down more information on Detective Calhoun. To repeat our top story—Abra Holloway has been found, safe and unharmed, in Illinois, although she has not yet offered any explanation for her disappearance. Stay tuned."

They knew everything. They knew about Sean. They knew exactly where she was. She rubbed her fist against her temple, trying to stop the pounding. It was what she had been most afraid of, and yet it still didn't seem real. But suddenly, as if they had just gotten more brave, somebody began to whale on the door and call out her name. The doorbell rang. *Ding dong, ding dong, ding dong.*

"Shut up!" she cried.

"Abra?" Sean appeared in the doorway, wearing just his jeans. "What the hell is going on?"

"Game over," she said bitterly, meeting his gaze. "There are a million reporters outside. We're trapped."

He edged behind the curtain, just as she had done, surveying the scene outside. "Not so good."

"What was your first hint?" she asked, her voice dripping with sarcasm.

"Sweetheart, it will be all right," he told her calmly.

Damn him, anyway, for being Mr. Chilly in the Face of Emergency. She wanted to see panic, damn it!

She wanted to see something approximating what she was feeling.

"We just issue a statement that we're in love, we're expecting, and we needed some time to ourselves. They ask about Julian, we say he's not a factor. And that's the end of it."

"It won't be all right," she managed between gritted teeth.

But he joined her on the sofa, still unruffled, trying to reassure her, to put his arm around her. But she brushed him off, even as he offered, "Abra, we'll figure it out."

"What is there to figure out?" she demanded, irate. "I can't speak to them yet. I can't get out of here. I'm stuck."

"Do you want me to go out and get rid of them?"

"There is no way to do that, Sean. More altercations? More ripped film and smashed cameras? All of them? I don't think so." She shook her head. "If you even try, you'll be blasted all over the news, too. I can see it now. Chicago Cop Caught In Love Nest With Abra Cadabra! That would be jolly, wouldn't it? Wreck both our careers."

"I can handle myself," he said slowly. "Or if you're not ready to talk to them yet, I can go out there, tell them we'll have a statement later, and they need to leave now."

"And you think they'll do it?"

"I don't much care if they do or not."

She stood up and began pacing back and forth. "I was better off by myself, before you got into this. I was better off hidden behind the sunglasses and the big coat, before you made me change my disguise. I should never have let you in. I told you not to contact anyone at the police department, but you just couldn't resist. And now look at what we're faced with."

"You're blaming me?"

"Listen to your phone messages, Sean! Good old Bill said that if you knew where I was, you could make good bucks off the info. So who do you think figured out where you were and with whom and sold the story?" Furious with his inability to see what was staring him in the face, she sent him a murderous glare. "You'll have to tell your pal Bill thanks for me for screwing up my life so beautifully."

Sean backed up, sticking his hands in his pockets. Pensive, he said, "I don't actually think it matters how the information got out, but no, I don't think it was Bill. My first guess would be the fact that somebody spotted you at last night's robbery attempt."

She hadn't thought about that. Why not? It was obvious. She'd just been so caught up in loving Sean she hadn't been paying attention. Still... "But I didn't give my name to anyone. No one saw me."

"Use your head, Abra," he said sharply. "Any one of the people who was there last night could have recognized you and called in a tip. I tried to keep you out of it, but I wasn't careful enough. I was—" he set his jaw "—distracted."

"No one saw me," she maintained stubbornly. "I think it was you talking about me to that Bill person. Or your mother. She could've spilled the beans, too, you know."

But Sean wasn't listening. "Plenty of people saw you, including the guy who took our photo in the parking lot, the one whose film I trashed."

"The reporter. Oh, no. Maybe it's in the paper." She didn't even remember picking it up, but it was over there, by the door, where she'd dropped it.

Retrieving it, she quickly glanced at the headlines. Nothing about her, although there was a story about the robbery and a small picture of Sean, being lauded as the hero. But nothing about her, no picture of the two of them kissing in the parking lot, nothing to suggest that anyone in Champaign-Urbana knew she was here or had contacted outside authorities. "No. Nothing about me. It had to be Bill or your mother."

"You still don't get it, do you?" he shot back. "It doesn't matter how the story broke. What matters is how you deal with it now."

She lifted her chin. "I have a right to know where the leak came from."

"Why? It all comes back to blaming me, anyway," Sean said acidly. "Bill, my mother, the robbery. Just think, even if it was because someone spotted you last night, if I'd only let that guy rob the place, shoot it up, whatever he had in mind, you might still be happily hiding out today. Of course, you also wouldn't have had the adrenaline high and the great roll in the hay. Cause and effect, you know. Small price to pay."

"Don't be ugly, Sean."

"I know you'll figure out a way for it to be my fault, Abra, one way or the other." He shook his head. "It's always someone else's fault, isn't it? Never mind that you're the one with all the secrets, the one running away instead of facing your mistakes straight on like an adult."

He was attacking her now? "That is really unfair."

"Don't you see? If you blame me, it gives you a perfect excuse to cut and run." Softly, persuasively, he added, "Don't do it, Abra. Stand up for once. You have a right to a life. Take it."

"I don't know yet what I'm going to do." But he had a point. It didn't make it any more pleasant, but he had a point. "I have to come up with a plan."

"You'd better decide soon." Sean took another surreptitious look out from behind the drapes. "They're getting restless out there."

"A plan," she mumbled, looking for her yellow pad. A list. She needed a list. "Should I draft a statement? But what do I say? There's no way to explain any of this. If I had answers, I could call a press conference. I could call it, anyway, and stonewall them and tell them it's none of their business, but that would be terrible PR. Sometimes it works if you just apologize all over the place. But what about my hair and my appearance?" She picked up a strand of choppy brown hair. "I can't be in public like this."

"Your hair and your appearance are what you're worried about?" Sean asked, his face a study in surprise. "Abra, do I know you at all?"

"Apparently not," she said stiffly. Who exactly did he think she was? Some small-town damsel in distress who could look like something the cat dragged in without anyone noticing? If she wanted her fans to forgive her and embrace her, she had to look like the Abra they knew and loved and respected. "Excuse me, but I have some things to attend to. I think I need to call Shelby and my manager. My press rep. Definitely my press rep. And Julian."

Mentioning Julian got his attention. "Your phone isn't working," he reminded her coldly.

"Yours is."

"Sure." Starting to steam a little around the edges, he pulled it out of his pocket. "Use my phone. Call Julian. Be sure to tell him the engagement is back on." Next he grabbed his wallet. "And here's all the cash I have. And take my ATM card, too, okay?" He stuffed money and cards into her hands. "Better take my car keys as well. Anything else I can do for you, Abra? Would you like me to throw myself off the roof to create a distraction while you run out the front door?"

"No need to be snide. I wasn't going to call him to get back together. You know that." She dumped his cell and his money back into his hands just as the phone began to ring again.

This time he answered it himself. "Yeah." He glanced at Abra. "Hi, Ma. No. I haven't been out this morning. Really? What did you say?"

Abra hovered, dying to hear the other end of the conversation.

"Okay. No biggie. No, I don't care. No, I am not in a love nest with Abra Holloway." He gave her a level stare. "I barely know her."

She felt a chill seep into her bones. *What do you expect, Abra? You made a mess for yourself, and everything fell apart just like you knew it would, and now you're blaming him. How did you expect him to react?*

"I think 'no comment' is probably your best bet.

Just keeping saying 'no comment' no matter how many times they call you. Or better yet, don't answer the phone." He flipped his cell phone shut. "Reporters have been all over my mother," he summed up tersely. "You were right. I believe the exact headline was Abra Caught In Love Nest With Boy-Toy Cop. So, you know, you were very close."

"How can you be so calm about this?" she asked, aghast. Boy-toy cop? It was worse than she'd expected. "Don't you care that within twenty-four hours you're going to be the punchline in Letterman's monologue?"

Sean lifted his bare shoulders. "Why should I care?"

"You don't care that the entire country will think you're some boy toy in a love nest?"

"Why should I care what other people think?"

"Because...because... You don't understand," she muttered. She wished *she* did.

"I understand better than you think." He advanced on her, storm clouds on his brow. "Everyone thinks you're perfect. But the baby and your relationship—if you can call it that—with Julian the Jerk are concrete evidence that you're not perfect at all." He paused. "That's it, isn't it? Abra Holloway doesn't want anyone to know that she's a big fat fake who makes as many mistakes as the schmoes who call in to *The Shelby Show* for advice."

Abra couldn't listen to any more of this. "Excuse me. I have to pack."

But he followed her, watching as she slapped all three of her Louis Vuitton bags onto the rumpled bed, grabbing clothes off hangers, smashing them into the suitcases.

"Damn it, Abra, look at me," he said angrily. "You can't just run away from me like you did Julian. Excuse me, but we slept together. That means something to me, even if it doesn't to you."

Stunned, she spun around. "Why would you think it doesn't mean anything to me?"

"Well, you're certainly ready to throw it away without a whimper. Which is exactly what you did to my boy Julian, now that I think about it." Crossing his arms over his chest, he spared her a cutting glance. "You obviously slept with him even though he wasn't that important. You'll forgive me for thinking maybe I'm not that important, either."

She couldn't help herself. Too much emotion, too many reversals. She whipped back and smacked him, hard. "You're defending Julian now? How dare you? You know what he put me through."

Sean stepped back, her handprint fading on his cheek. "Abra, you're the one who agreed to marry the guy. You're the one who cared enough to make a baby with him. Sooner or later you're going to have to realize that some of this is your responsibility, too."

"I was *not* going to marry him," she shot back. "Engaged and married are very different things."

"Excuse me?"

"It was not a love match, okay? I already told you that!" She was so livid she couldn't see straight. To think that she had been so thrilled Sean was on her side. Ha! He was defending *Julian*. "I admit, I went into it with my eyes open, because, well, I was tired of being lonely after all those years, and I thought having someone in my life—no strings, no real intimacy, but a perfect escort for my arm at the Emmys—was the smart way to go. I was bound and determined not to make the same mistake I did the first time, with David. So this time I hooked up with Julian because he was distant and unavailable and I didn't have to hand over my heart."

"Abra, you don't have to explain to me—"

"Yes. I do. I didn't love Julian for one minute and I don't want you to think that I did. But I made a mistake. I had sex with him." Wound up, ready to let loose, she couldn't stop herself. "Twice. Yes, that's right. Exactly twice."

"That's all?"

"What, you don't believe me, either?" she railed. "The first time was because, hey, we were engaged and we'd been to a lovely party and I had a little too much to drink—"

"You'll forgive me if I don't want to hear the details," he interjected.

"There are no details." Head high, she crossed her arms, too, trying to look strong and unbowed. "I just wanted to know if we were at all compatible. And the second time was just because I wanted to see if the first time—as pale and boring as it was—was the way it would always be. It was. But lo and behold, I turned up pregnant. Except, as you know, he doesn't believe it's his."

"Abra, calm down," he tried. "I am not taking his side. He is a jerk. No question."

She hugged her arms, feeling very cold and alone.

"Isn't it great to be Abra Holloway, who tells everybody else what to do, whose life is such a joke that she has to drag the father of her baby to court because he apparently thinks she sleeps with everyone but the grocery boy? Or maybe he includes the grocery boy. I don't know." She laughed. "Guess you'd have to ask Julian."

"I don't ever want to see Julian, let alone ask him anything," Sean said roughly. "Isn't it bad enough he fathered your baby?"

"But that's what I'm looking at when I walk out and face those reporters, Sean. That's what they're going to ask me and yell at me," she tried to explain. "Now that I've been caught in a love nest with my boy-toy cop, it even looks like Julian was right. He's going to come off as the wronged man, while I'm the big slut who set up housekeeping with another guy she just met. People may think the baby is yours, Sean. They may think it's the grocery boy's. I just don't know. Don't you see that?"

"So let him do his worst," he returned. "I'm not afraid. I'll stand by you, Abra. Right by your side. Whatever happens. So what if people think this baby is mine? It's more mine than Julian's at this point. Doesn't that count for something?"

"Loyal to a fault." She let out a huge sigh of despair. "I couldn't do that to you. And I couldn't do that to my career. It will all come out now, you know. The screwed-up marriage when I was nineteen, the screwed-up, semi-fake engagement, and twice, such terrible decisions about the men I chose to get involved with! And now somewhere along the line, I've picked up number three. How do I explain that? How do I explain *you?*"

"You don't. You say, this is what it is. Sean is who he is. We are together. Now deal."

Things were so easy for him, so black and white. Her shoulders slumped. "But they won't deal. They'll slice and dice me instead. They'll start counting the months and asking questions. And if I don't come up with answers, my career will be up in smoke."

"Abra, if your career is a lie," he argued, "what does it matter if it goes up in smoke? You're smart, you're talented, and you will find something to do even if you're not Abra Cadabra."

"You don't understand." She looked down at the fabulous aloe-green Gucci suit lying next to her fabulous Louis Vuitton valise. And then she glanced back up at Sean. "I *want* to be Abra Cadabra."

"So what was this?" he asked, stung. "Slumming it for a while? Using me for what I was worth and then throwing me away?"

"No. But..." But what? *But I made another really bad choice, Sean, and you were it?* "I think it was like time out of mind," she pleaded. "Like being somebody else for a while. And it was really good, Sean, but I just don't know who that is."

"I don't, either." Bleakly, he added, "And since I seem to be the fall guy, I'm not sure I care. I guess you've convinced me you're right not to fight for us. There was no us, was there?"

As he turned, stalking out of the bedroom, slamming the door, Abra held her breath. "It's better this way," she told herself out loud. "You knew you were going to have to face the music by yourself sooner or later. At least maybe this way, Sean won't have to go down with you."

Methodically, she began to fold and pack her belongings into the largest bag. She shut it and fastened it. Then she started on the rest.

She had almost finished by the time he came back. "Nobody has moved outside," he informed her. "How were you planning to get out of here through the circus?"

"I don't know." She started to drag her bags toward the door.

"You'd better figure out something."

"I'll call a cab. I'll put on my hat and my big coat and keep my head down." Abra found a semblance of a smile. "The pictures will look dandy on the news. They can call me disheveled again."

"Listen, we can do better than that. I'll leave, take your suitcases, and put then in my car," he offered. "Then I can circle around for a while. Hopefully they'll follow me, and give you time to sneak out the back. Once you think the back way is clear, you just head straight through, and I'll pick you up on the next street. Okay?"

"Sean, you don't need to—"

"Don't worry. My help has been so lousy so far, I'll throw this last rescue in for free. If I can just find my shirt..." He began to search around the bed. "Have you seen my shirt from last night? Black T-shirt?"

"Oh." She stopped where she was, set the big suitcase on its side, and opened the lid. It took a second to unearth his T-shirt, but she found it. "Here it is. Sorry."

"You took my shirt?"

"It was an accident," she contended. "It just...got stuck in with my things. I was packing, I wasn't paying attention, and it got swept up." Feeling defensive, she finished up with, "I said it was an accident."

"Right." He shrugged into the shirt.

So what if she'd wanted something that smelled like him to take with her? So what if she was weak and ridiculous?

It only seemed fair to take something with her. After all, she was leaving her heart.

HIS RESCUE PLAN WORKED like a dream, but he didn't say a word to her all the way to the rental car place. He rented the car, handed over the keys, and even opened the door for her. And then she was on her way. Alone. Unencumbered. Without some arrogant man telling her what to do. "That is the way I want it," she kept repeating.

She got as far as O'Hare airport before her resolve started to crumble. She was tired, she was hungry, and she was already so lonely she thought she might die. *Damn it.* If Sean had been with her on that three-hour car trip, they would've been arguing about pizza and ice cream and having a great time. This way, she got to decide what to eat when she wanted to with no interference, but what did it get her?

She had been so sure she needed to go back to New York by herself, to put her people together and come up with some strategy for a painless reentry into society. Which was exactly what she had been doing since she left it, without a bit of success.

Doomed for failure, one more time.

"Sean is right," she whispered, dropping her luggage in front of the skycap. "About everything."

There was no strategy. There was only the truth.

She wanted to call him. Should she call him?

No.

Instead, she grabbed her bags back from the skycap before they disappeared. "Where's a telephone?" she demanded. "Do they even have pay phones anymore?"

He pointed inside, and she hauled her three bags along as best she could, rolling along, desperate for a phone. "Credit card, credit card," she muttered, fumbling with her purse to find the right card and her address book, with her press rep's number in it. How strange. She was feeling butterflies to call her press agent. "Hello, Maria? It's Abra. I'm back. No, not in New York. Chicago. Yeah, I know about the press and I'm going to try to handle that. Preemptive strike, you know. Good. I have some things to do on this end, but I need you to set up a press conference for me. Can you do that?"

Abra chewed her lip, staring out at the busy airport commuters. She certainly hoped this worked. "No, not in New York. In Chicago..."

13

SEAN TOOK HIS TIME cleaning out his hotel room, carefully torching all the surveillance pictures he'd taken of Abra, and then finally driving back to Chicago the next day. It wasn't like he wanted to go home. He was sure that whatever awaited him there wasn't going to be pretty. Besides, he preferred to think that Abra would be well out of the vicinity before he got back there.

"Don't need to hear that," he said out loud, switching off the radio before he heard the Abra Holloway story one more time. He had it memorized. *She's been found, managed to evade reporters at the love nest, no statement thus far, one expected shortly...* Yadda, yadda, yadda. It all added up to Abra still dithering around about what kind of statement she wanted to make. Or maybe she just needed a makeover before she faced the cameras.

Sean forced himself to think about something else. Anything else. Which sent him to the reason he had started this trip. Which wasn't any more pleasant than why he was ending it.

"So Cooper found the tootsie with the 'ho shoes," he groused. "I fail on that score, plus I get the worst publicity in the history of the Calhoun family. Hey, good job, Sean. Make your dad proud just when he's going for that big promotion. Sorry, Dad. Hope my new boy-toy-in-the-tabloids status doesn't kill your chances to be First Deputy."

Was he bitter? Why, yes, he was.

His reverie was interrupted by the insistent buzz of his cell phone. "I thought I turned that damn thing off."

He recognized the number. Without waiting to hear her voice, he said impatiently, "Mom, I'm almost home. I should be there within the hour, okay? So stop calling."

"I will not stop calling!" she snapped back at him. "Sean, you don't talk that way to your mother."

"Sorry." He waited for a second. "Well, are you going to tell me? What is it, Ma?"

"Don't go home," she whispered in a conspiratorial tone. "You should not go home, Sean. Not to your place and not the house, either."

"Why not?"

"The reporters. They've got satellite trucks and everything, all around our house. And Cooper said they're at your place, too." She speeded up when she said, "Like when the wagons circle around. There's a million of them. You don't want to walk into that hornets' nest."

Circling the wagons full of hornets' nests. Right. "Maybe I'll just keep driving. Wisconsin sounds good. Where's Jake? Is anybody at the fishing cabin?"

"No! You can't go there."

"Why?" He didn't like driving and using the

phone at the same time, and he was ready for this conversation to be over.

"Jake's got a new girlfriend. They're there. Kind of romantic and all. You don't want to interrupt."

"Jake's got a new girlfriend?" What, had the world turned upside-down? Where did Jake find a girlfriend that fast, especially one who wanted to go to a fishing cabin? "Okay, not the fishing cabin. You got somewhere else in mind?"

"I'm at Bebe's salon," she said coyly. "How about you come here?"

"Bebe's?" He hated Bebe's hair salon, always packed with chatty women, always heavy with the smell of permanents and lotions and hairspray. "Nah. I'll go home. Let the hornets circle."

"No, you can't. You need to come here, to Bebe's. I didn't want to tell you, but your girlfriend is going to be on *Entertainment Tonight*," she told him quickly. "At six-thirty."

Now he began to see where this was going. "My girlfriend?" he asked with a feeling of dread.

"Your Abra girl. Bebe says she saw the commercial. Tonight, she'll be on."

"She's not mine and she's not a girl." And he had no desire to see her chatting with some smarmy host about her plans for her new show as she also apologized out the wazoo for every imaginary transgression. *Sorry I'm pregnant. Sorry I left. Sorry I was mean to Julian. I've come back to my senses.* He couldn't stomach one minute of that.

Of course, there was the possibility that she had finally come to her senses and figured out where to go from here. But he doubted it. She'd had long enough to sort things through in Champaign, and she hadn't even come close. What was the likelihood she had gone through an epiphany now?

"Bebe has the big TV for customers to watch, so we're going to watch together," his mother offered. "I want to see this girl who's ruined my son's life."

"Ma, she didn't ruin anything." *I was stupid. I pushed in where I didn't belong, and I fell for someone I knew I could never have. Mea culpa.*

"So, Sean, it's all set," she finished up, clearly not listening to a word he was saying. "You come here and we'll watch it together and, you know, cushion the blow. You should be with family, Sean. Which is where you should be when you have heartbreak and misery and unhappiness."

Gee, she painted such a nice picture of his life. "What if I don't want to see her on *Entertainment Tonight*? What if I don't want to put myself through that?"

"Pffft. You want to see her. You know you do. It's her first big hoopdedoo press thingee since she surfaced. You're dying to hear what she has to say to explain all this. Not to mention what she says about you," she said hotly. "She utters one harsh word about my boy, and I will personally fly out to wherever she is and slap her silly."

"You will not."

"You need to hear her," she coaxed. "I know you,

hon. You don't leave a scab hanging that needs to be ripped off."

"Mom," he protested. That was gross.

"Listen, I gotta go, Sean. You come right here, you hear me? Bebe's salon. I expect to see you within the hour. Or," she threatened, "I'll tell your dad to send a squad car to pick you up. I know where you are. And I'll do it, too, Sean. You know I will."

"I know you will," he echoed with resignation. "I'll be right there."

THEY HADN'T TOLD HIM they were throwing a party. Bebe and his mother had brought in drinks and hors d'oeuvres for the big *Entertainment Tonight* extravaganza, and while Bebe continued to see customers, there was a steady flow of conversation, laughter, and noshing on shrimp toast and crab dip. They were sitting in the pink and purple chairs, under the turquoise dryers, on every possible pastel surface, all chattering and laughing and clinking martini glasses.

He knew there was a reason he hated Bebe's salon.

But he had to admit, the craziness did keep his mind off the fact that Abra was going to appear on the television over their heads any minute now. The program kept running teasers ("Abra Holloway comes clean! America wants to know where she's been and who she's been with. Wait till you hear Abra's red-hot secret!") every five seconds, every time they went to commercial, but they never actually seemed to get to the real interview.

"When is this thing going to be on?" Sean asked

again, not really expecting an answer. The salon patrons, from one with aluminum foil in her hot pink hair to the one with a green facial mask, kept whispering amongst themselves and peering at him, but they didn't actually talk to him. He knew the reason they were so curious was not just because he was the only guy in the place, but because they had seen his mug in the *Sun* and the *Star* and wanted to know what the scoop was.

His picture was all over the tabloids and the entertainment shows, now that he was unofficially Abra Holloway's boy-toy cop. He admitted it—he'd looked, just to see how bad the coverage was. And it was bad.

Just as she had predicted, he was even in a late night monologue. *Maybe she's going to collect a whole set of boy-toy action figures,* the host had quipped. *The policeman, the cowboy, the fireman...*

But his favorite was the schlocky tabloid that pasted his head on the body of some Hollywood version of a uniformed officer—someone who was a lot chunkier than Sean—just to make the point that he was one of the boys in blue, a man of the people, picked right off the street to be Abra's boy toy. Too bad he hadn't worn a uniform in years, ever since he made detective.

Accuracy was clearly not their strong suit. Abra had tried to warn him they would be barbecued, and she was right. He shouldn't have tried to dictate to her about her own industry. When it came to the fame game, Abra knew best.

Moody, wishing he was anywhere rather than here, Sean took a slug from a bottle of beer thoughtfully provided by Bebe. It was his third. Or maybe fourth. But he definitely needed the fortification. They'd also put him in the cushiest chair, and every time he tried to rise out of it, either Bebe or his mother or one of the other stylists came by and slapped him back down. Apparently, they were all on orders to keep him on a short leash. What were they so afraid of? He didn't have anywhere to be. If he had, he would've been there.

He glanced at the clock again. Maybe he could still get out of here without his mother noticing before Abra's piece came up.

Aw, who was he kidding? He wanted to see. He needed to see. His mother knew him only too well. But did he have to do it at a beauty parlor with a passel of women staring at him?

"Yvonne's son?" he heard more than once. "Is he really making it with that Abra Cadabra from TV?"

"I heard they were secretly married. But Yvonne says no."

"He's very cute. She could do worse."

"He's too good for her, I say."

Even on a good day, he did not appreciate being the center of conversation. This was not a good day.

The clock overhead said that there were only a few minutes left in the show. Were they going to get to her or not?

And once they did, what was she going to say?

"Oh, there she is!" someone shouted. "There she is! Coming up next!"

"I still say she looks an awful lot like the one from the park," Bebe complained. "You stick sunglasses and a scarf on her, and she's a dead ringer."

"Oh, she is not!" his mom shot back. "This one is much prettier and classier."

Prettier and classier, but she was going to fly out to wherever she was and slap her? He never would understand his mother.

"I'd like to get my hands on her hair," Bebe said with spirit. "She'd be a whole lot prettier with that mop cut and styled right."

"Shh," Yvonne Calhoun interrupted, waving her hands at Bebe. "Look, she's on now and we can't hear her. Turn it up! Turn it up!" She came swooping over and poked him. "Sean, are you watching?"

"What else would I be doing?"

"Don't be a smarty." She poked him again. "Pay attention."

"So, Abra," the unctuous blond interviewer began. "Can you tell us why you left *The Shelby Show* in such a hurry? What was that all about?"

"It's very easy to explain, really," Abra said sweetly. She was wearing part of that green suit they'd had the argument about, the one she said was Gucci or Pucci or something important. She had the jacket over a different dress, but he had to admit, she looked great in it.

She smiled into the camera, and it felt like she was looking right at him. How did she do that so easily?

Even with the choppy brown hair, even knowing she was in deep, dark water, she still had so much confidence, and every bit of the trademark Abra Cadrabra warmth and energy and spark. Seeing her up there on that big screen, he wanted her all over again. He felt like he'd been sucker-punched.

"Uh-huh." The interviewer tipped her blond vapid head to one side, pretending to be listening intently. "Tell me more, Abra."

"I needed some time to myself," Abra announced, looking very sincere. "I found myself at a crossroad, and I felt I needed to take my time, away from the pressures of the show, to really reflect."

"Now you told us you needed time alone. But you were with someone, weren't you?" The blonde was trying for a just-us-girls approach that seemed really silly on national TV. "A certain hunk of a Chicago police detective, isn't that right? We've heard he saved your life from a crazed gunman, Abra. Was that before or after the two of you fell in love?"

Abra took a short pause. He could see the wheels turning, as every woman in Bebe's salon leaned forward expectantly, holding their collective breath. But Abra said, "That's really not what I'm here to talk about."

"Ohh," they all exhaled in disappointment, sending Sean their most sympathetic looks.

Hey, he wasn't complaining. If she didn't want to talk about him, so much the better. He started to rise, but his mother and Bebe both leapt forward. "Sit down!" they chorused.

"Okay, okay, I'm sitting."

"What I do want to talk about is that I am expecting a baby," Abra said serenely.

Every jaw in the salon hit the black-and-white tiled floor.

"So you can understand why my life needed to go through some changes, and why I now need to concentrate on personal matters. I had hoped to launch my own show next year, but I will be launching a family instead." And her smiled widened. She looked so happy about the baby that he couldn't help smiling, too.

"Sean." His mother smacked him on the arm. "How could you? You didn't tell me she was pregnant. That poor girl!"

He kept his mouth shut. But there were a whole lot of accusing eyes pointed his way. They all swiveled back around to the TV when Abra began to speak again.

"While I am really sorry to bid goodbye to *The Shelby Show* and my dear friend Shelby Marino, I am really excited about what's ahead for me."

"Who's the father, Abra?" the ET interviewer asked hotly. "America wants to know. Is it your fiancé Julian? Or the detective who saved your life?"

Again, she hesitated. Again, a pin could've dropped in the salon. "This is better than *The Young and the Restless*," hissed one woman with her hair in rollers.

"Shh," everybody else said in unison.

"The biological father is not an issue." Abra's

cheeks grew pink. Uh-oh. She was having a tougher time of it. So far, he was giving her major points for honesty and discretion, but what would she say next? "I would like to say that there is someone important in my life. Very important." Now she gazed straight into the camera, selling her words as if her life depended on it. Sean was pretty sure at this point that his life did depend on it.

"Say it, Abra," Sean begged under his breath.

"If he'll have me, I hope we can build this family together."

There was a whoosh of romantic appreciation in the crowd around him. "Does she mean Sean?" one of the hair stylists asked quietly.

"Of course she does. Who else?" his mother demanded.

He wished he was that sure. At the moment, he was more numb than anything else. He took another long draw from the beer bottle, happy to have something to do while his brain raced. Was she talking about him? If not, who? But why didn't she come right out and say so?

On the screen, as the reporter tried to press the point, Abra was adamant. "That's all I'm going to say. I don't think this is anyone's business but mine." She smiled demurely. "And I hope one other person's."

The blonde kept firing away, pestering Abra with questions about the baby, about Julian, about Sean and the love nest and the robbery, and especially about her future. He wanted to throttle the bimbo.

What did she think this was, *Sixty Minutes*? But Abra held her own, sticking to her main points, refusing to divulge anything she didn't want to.

"Don't your fans deserve to know the truth?" the blonde interrogated. "You left them in the lurch, Abra. And now you make this shocking announcement, but refuse to go any further. Doesn't America deserve to hear a more complete story from Abra Holloway, of all people?"

"I'm sorry if I've disappointed anyone who believed I had all the answers or that my life was perfect. Clearly I do not and it is not." Speaking clearly and distinctly, she raised her chin and blazed them with that trademark sparkly Abra smile. "I will fully understand if my fans are unhappy or if they decide not to follow me into new ventures. At the moment, I'm not sure there will be new ventures to follow me into. But I decided that there were some things more important than my public image."

Sean could feel a major grin curving his lips. "That's my girl," he whispered. Abra had come to her senses.

"Well?" his mom inquired, raising an eyebrow. "What are you going to do about it, Sean? That poor girl is pregnant and alone and she practically comes out and proposes to you on national television. What are you going to do about it?"

"Woo-hoo!" He'd never made that noise before in his life, but there it was, coming out of his mouth. Before he stopped to think, he grabbed his mother and twirled her around in the air.

"Sean! Put me down!" she squealed. "You have better things to do than torment your mother."

"You're right. I've got to get to the airport as soon as I can," he said in a rush. As soon as he set her down, she glared at him. Fluffing her hair back into place, she took off for the back of the salon, where the hair dryers were.

But he didn't have time for whatever bee was in his mother's bonnet. "Anybody here a travel agent?" he asked the collection of ladies. "Anybody have an opinion as to whether Midway or O'Hare could get me out quicker? I've got to get to New York. I've got to get to Abra."

"Why do you think she's in New York?" Bebe asked, arching her pencil-thin eyebrow. "I think that show is filmed in L.A."

There were lots of nods around her.

"L.A.?" Abra would never go to Los Angeles just to film that stupid show. She'd have picked one in New York instead. Except he suddenly realized they'd never actually shown the interviewer and Abra in the same frame. In fact, they seemed completely separate. "Did she do that interview by remote? They do this stuff by satellite all the time, don't they?"

Now the women in the salon were starting to giggle.

"What?" Sean was confused and dazed and feeling in way over his head. What were they all giggling about? A few too many martinis? He liked having a goal and going for it, not standing around a beauty

salon gabbing with the good-time girls. Meanwhile...
"How do I find out where she is?"

"Surprise!" Bebe cried. "We got you good, Sean!"

"What exactly do you mean?"

The salon patrons began to part, edging toward the walls, opening up a space for his mother.

"Look, look, here she is!" Yvonne Calhoun sang out, dragging someone out from under a hair dryer near the back of the salon.

He couldn't seem to find his voice. "Abra?" he choked.

As she stood up, he could see that she was the right size, the right shape, and she had the right gorgeous hazel eyes, full of warmth and energy and sparkle. Her hair was a lot lighter, cut shorter but even and smooth, and she was wearing a beige sleeveless top with white pants and gold hoop earrings. All simple, but classy. He'd never seen her with golden blond hair or soft makeup or expensive clothes, and he honestly had no idea if these fell into that category, anyway. But she looked beautiful. Whether she'd shown up wrapped head to foot in gauze or the world's most fabulous evening gown, he didn't care. He was just so damn glad to see her.

"She wasn't sure you would want to see her," his mom noted, clucking her tongue as she pulled Abra along by the hand. But she seemed reluctant, shy, and she hesitated, just standing there, out of reach. "Once you dumped her in a rental car and sent her packing—"

"I didn't—"

Once again, his mother cut him off. "She told me all about it, Sean. Poor thing. But she decided to stay here in Chicago for a little while, and she called me, and she told me everything. Well, almost everything." She grumbled, "Not about this baby."

"Mom—"

"I know, I know, it's none of my business. But if I had known about that, I really would've been pushy." She shook her head from side to side. "You don't just let a poor pregnant girl who needs you walk out of your life, Sean. Haven't I taught you better than that?"

"Mom—"

"No excuses. It all turned out fine, didn't it?" she said happily. "So I talked her into staying and letting Bebe take that awful brown out of her hair and cut it better. So now here she is, beautiful again, and ready to see you. So? Sean?"

She gave Abra a push in his direction, and he was happy to catch her.

"What, Mom?"

"So kiss the girl already!"

God, she felt good in his arms. Why wasn't she saying anything? Maybe because his mother wasn't allowing anyone else to get a word in edgewise.

Abra tugged on his sleeve, tipping her head near his. "Sean, if this isn't what you want..." she whispered.

"How could I not want you?"

"But I'm serious." She certainly looked serious. Leave it to Abra to overthink and overanalyze, even while being steamrolled by his matchmaking mother. "I know I said some terrible things and I acted like a big baby," Abra added in that same slow, cautious voice, "and I don't want you to think you have to go along with this, or to take me in, just because I don't have anywhere else to go or because your mother is so gung-ho." She peeked around his shoulder. "And now that she knows about the baby, how gung-ho is she going to be?"

"You're kidding, right?" His hands framed her face, and his eyes searched hers.

"That didn't come out right. I meant to say that you have some legitimate objections and arguments, and I want you to be able to raise those," she offered. "I mean, I'm having a baby that we both know isn't yours, and that is a serious thing which we should've talked about before, you know, we got so involved, but I was so smitten and I wanted you so much... And I still do!"

"Good." He closed his eyes and pressed his lips to hers, fierce and strong and possessive. "Because you're stuck with me for a really long time." He kissed her again. "Like forever."

"You're sure this is what you want?" she asked softly. "Me? The baby? I don't know what I'm going to do or where I go from here. I don't have a job, I do have a baby, and I am kind of a pain sometimes."

"I'm sure." He glanced back at his mother, who was practically beside herself to see her son matched up. "And so is my mom."

"You're sure?"

"Abra, if I tell you I'm sure, I'm sure." He grinned and held her as tight as he could manage. "I'm a True Blue Calhoun, remember? My word is my bond."

And then he sighed with joy and relief that the nightmare was over. Abra was his. He was hers. And it was going to stay that way.

*   *   *   *   *

Next month look for the final book in
The True Blue Calhouns
miniseries by popular Julie Kistler

#965 PACKING HEAT

Cooper, the last of the sexy Calhoun brothers, is still on the hunt for the mysterious Toni. While pursuing a hot lead he runs straight into FBI agent Violet O'Leary. She isn't thrilled when Coop suddenly interferes with her case. *Could it be they are after the same person?* Worse, Coop keeps trying to distract Violet—by kissing her, seducing her and handcuffing her to his brass bed! What will happen next is anyone's guess...

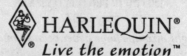

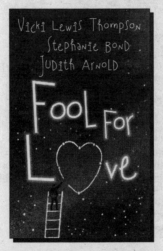
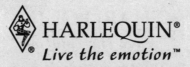

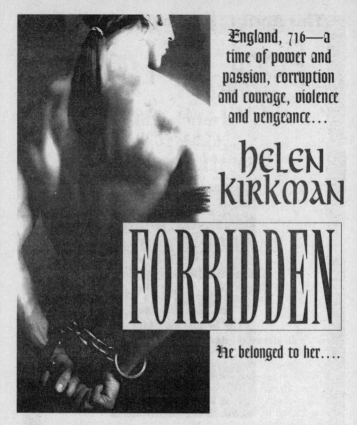
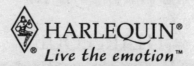

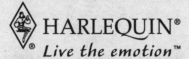